DOWN TO EARTH

DOWN TO EARTH

BETTY CULLEY

CROWN BOOKS FOR YOUNG READERS
NEW YORK

Text copyright © 2021 by Betty Culley
Jacket art copyright © 2021 by Robert Frank Hunter

All rights reserved. Published in the United States by Crown Books for Young Readers, an imprint of Random House Children's Books, a division of Penguin Random House LLC, New York.

Crown and the colophon are registered trademarks of Penguin Random House LLC.

Visit us on the Web! rhcbooks.com

Educators and librarians, for a variety of teaching tools, visit us at RHTeachersLibrarians.com

Library of Congress Cataloging-in-Publication Data
Names: Culley, Betty, author.
Title: Down to earth / Betty Culley.
Description: First edition. | New York: Crown Books for Young Readers, [2021] | Audience: Ages 8-12. | Audience: Grades 4-6. | Summary: Ten-year-old aspiring geologist Henry Bower investigates the meteorite that crash lands in the hayfield, discovering a rock that will change his family, his town, and even himself.
Identifiers: LCCN 2020050620 (print) | LCCN 2020050621 (ebook) | ISBN 978-0-593-17573-6 (hardcover) | ISBN 978-0-593-17574-3 (library binding) | ISBN 978-0-593-17575-0 (ebook)
Subjects: CYAC: Meteorites—Fiction. | Family life—Fiction. | Dowsing—Fiction. | Change—Fiction.
Classification: LCC PZ7.1.C832 Dow 2021 (print) | LCC PZ7.1.C832 (ebook) | DDC [Fic]—dc23

The text of this book is set in 12.5-point Apollo MT.
Interior design by Katrina Damkoehler

Printed in Italy
10 9 8 7 6 5 4 3 2 1
First Edition

FOR MY DAUGHTER, RACHEL

CHAPTER ONE

The pointed end of a forked stick is believed to point
toward the ground when it passes over water.
—*THE WORLD BOOK ENCYCLOPEDIA: VOLUME D*

WHEN I WAS FIVE, I watched my father saw a Y-shaped twig off my great-grandfather's hundred-year-old apple tree. I waited to see if he would cut any other letters. There were branches that would make good L's and I's and a curved J just right for my best friend, James. I wondered if Dad would saw off three branches and tie them together to make the H for my name—Henry.

Now I'm one hundred percent older than I was then, and when Dad circles the tree his grandfather planted on Bower Hill Road, I know he's not looking for letters. He's searching for the perfect forked stick for dowsing. He doesn't dowse for buried metal or gemstones. My dad, Harlan Bower, is a water dowser, and he uses his stick to find veins of water deep underground.

It doesn't have to be apple wood. It can be pear or willow. But if I ever try to dowse for real, I want my first branch to come from my great-grandfather's tree.

Having an H name like my father doesn't make me a dowser.

Being a Bower doesn't make me a dowser.

Living on Bower Hill Road, with its underground springs and good-tasting well water, doesn't make me a dowser.

My great-grandfather and grandfather could find fresh water trapped beneath hard granite rock.

Sixty-six-point-sixty-six percent of my grandfather's sons are dowsers.

My father: 33.33 percent
Uncle Lincoln: 33.33 percent
Uncle Braggy: 0 percent

My grandfather, my father, and Uncle Lincoln all discovered their water dowser talents when they were ten. I already read about dowsing in the D encyclopedia. It tells what it is, but not why some people can do it and other people can't.

My father taught me how to dig a hole with straight sides and how to put rubble rocks in the middle of my stone walls so they can shift with the frost.

But when I asked him how to dowse, he said it's not something you can teach, it just happens.

I asked which was more important, the stick or the person that held it, and he said both.

I asked if it was easier to dowse for water on a rainy day, and he said he'd never thought about that.

The apple tree has a black gash on the trunk where lightning hit it. No one saw the lightning strike, and the tree kept growing. No one teaches a tree to find water. Its taproot goes straight down into the earth, the same direction my father's dowsing stick bends when it finds water.

The day I turned ten, I went up the hill and stood under my great-grandfather's tree. It was late August and there were so many apples they pulled the branches down around me. I touched the gash where lightning marked the tree. When I looked up, all I could see were Y's. Big Y's, little Y's, straight and crooked, too many to count. I traced the straightest Y with my finger, but I didn't break it off the tree.

This perfect Y is at the very end of a branch that grows toward Nana's front porch. It will be an easy one to find again if Dad asks me to dowse for a well. Then I'll finally learn whether my great-grandfather's abilities were passed down to me or not.

If I could have chosen to be a dowser for my tenth birthday present, I would have, but I know Dad would say it's not something anyone else can give you.

CHAPTER TWO

Dowsing (water witching or water divining)
is probably as old as man's need for water.
It is an "art" certain people have which enables
them to find underground sources of water.
—Joseph Baum, *The Beginner's Handbook*
of Dowsing: The Ancient Art of
Divining Underground Water Sources

BEFORE WE HEAD OUT into the icy field, James breaks a branch off a wild cherry tree for his dowsing stick. I pull my little sister, Birdie, behind us on her red sled. It's so cold out the snow that falls is gritty like sand and won't stick. It's the kind my father calls dry snow.

James holds the Y-shaped branch the way my father and Uncle Lincoln do when they dowse—palms up, each hand holding an end of the V, elbows at his sides, the end of the Y pointing out in front of him.

"What should I dowse for, Henry?" James asks me. "A mammoth tusk like the one we saw in the museum?"

"How about Dad's good hammer? He lost it at the top of the field when he was fixing the tractor last summer."

"Then I'll dowse in that direction." James's eyes are the clear blue of the sky reflected in the ice, and his blond hair sticks out from under his wool hat.

"*Keek keek keek*." A small hawk glides overhead.

"*Keek keek*," Birdie calls back. Birdie is only two, but she can make a cry just like a hawk.

"*Keek keek keek*," the hawk screeches again, and flies off into the thick woods at the edge of the field.

"I think I see something!" James yells, running ahead with his branch. "Look! A deer antler! My best find yet!" He holds up the antler. "I bet this would sell fast on the yard sale table."

James brings over the antler, and Birdie and I touch the hard, bony points.

Then Birdie starts wiggling her legs in the sled.

"Slide down," she says.

"Can you say 'Push my sled, Henry'?"

I try to get Birdie to say more than two words at a time and to say my name in the sentence.

"SLIDE NOW," Birdie tells me.

I start her sled with a gentle push, and as it picks up speed, Birdie puts her arms out like wings. The dry snow makes the sled squeak.

"You're going fast, Birdie. Hold on to the sides!" I shout. "Steer toward the hay bales!"

Dad puts hay bales at the bottom of the hill to stop our sleds so we don't slide out into the road. I watch Birdie zoom down the hill, the red of her mittens two bright spots moving in the air.

"I DO!" Birdie shouts back.

She doesn't steer with her hands, but she leans her body from side to side, like a hawk in the air.

"Here, Henry." James gives me his dowsing stick. "You take it. You're the real dowser. I'm gonna go up in the woods and see if I can knock down some pinecones for your mom to start fires with."

He's sure I'm a dowser even though I haven't dowsed for real. The last time I went with Dad on a well-drilling job, I offered to try dowsing. When I said that, Dad stood still for a second, staring at me, and answered, *Lincoln could use a hand digging the drainage ditch.* Which didn't make sense, because you don't dig the ditch until you find the spot to drill. And you don't find the spot to drill until you dowse for it.

I think he didn't want to watch me try and try and not be able to do it. Or hear what people in town would say when they heard what happened: *Too bad that Bower boy can't dowse like his father.*

James runs across the ice, as excited about getting pinecones for Mom as he was about finding the antler. I once heard my father say it was wonderful how James gave one hundred percent to whatever he was doing. Especially since he almost drowned with his mother when he was Birdie's age.

I stared at my father when he said that, not because of what he said about James's mother. Everyone in Lowington knows she died throwing James to safety on Eagle Lake when her snowmobile broke through thin ice. But because I thought maybe that was where I got my percent thinking from.

Like here out in our field, I'm twenty percent wondering if dowsers are born with special hearing or smell senses that help them find water. I've only got seven more months, until I turn eleven, to figure out what makes someone a dowser. I'm thinking when I get back home, I'll look in the encyclopedias my uncle Braggy gave me. Which volume would I look in? S for sense or H for hearing or W for water? Or maybe the Lowington library has a book about it. Before I know it, I am forty percent thinking about James and Birdie, and sixty percent thinking about the way dowsers find things.

"And me? How many percent for me?" I wanted to know when Dad said one hundred percent about James.

"You?" My father looked at me then like he was seeing me for the first time. I have my father's straight black hair and long legs like all the Bowers except Uncle Braggy, and Birdie and I both have my mother's mossy eyes. Mom calls them mossy because they're the greenish brown, brownish green of the moss that grows on our stone walls.

"You are one hundred percent Henry," he said.

Which is not exactly an answer. Who else could I be?

Birdie's sled bumps into a hay bale right before the road, and I hold James's dowsing stick out the way I've seen my father and Uncle Lincoln do a hundred times. Then a strange thing happens there on the frozen hill. For a second, I think I feel the forked branch pull upward toward the sky instead of down the way my father's dowsing stick moves, but I can't be sure if it's the branch moving or my cold hands shaking.

CHAPTER THREE

If you are a dowser and you pass over an underground water supply, the end of the stick will suddenly be pulled downward to a vertical position.
—JOSEPH BAUM, *THE BEGINNER'S HANDBOOK OF DOWSING*

OUR TOWN LIBRARY has two books about dowsing and one book about water. The brick building covered with vines is next to James's school on Main Street in Lowington. The shelves go right up to the ceiling, and a metal ladder slides back and forth on a track. Mrs. Kay, the librarian, lets me climb for my books.

"Red book." Birdie points to a book with red leather binding halfway up the wall. "Climb up."

There's a section in the corner of the library with children's books that are easy to reach, but Birdie picks her books by their color or their size. She likes the biggest ones or the ones with red covers, and especially books that are big and red.

Mrs. Kay lets Birdie climb the ladder, too, as long as I'm behind her, although I don't think Birdie really needs my help. She's never been afraid of heights. Once she began walking, instead of digging for rocks like me or looking for things on the ground like Mom, Birdie surprised everyone by turning her face to the sky.

"Got it." Birdie pulls the red book off the shelf and climbs back down with one hand on the ladder and one hand holding the book. She puts it on Mrs. Kay's desk. Mrs. Kay is not much taller than I am, and when she sits behind the big wooden desk, she looks even smaller.

"*The Arabian Nights*! Good choice, Birdie." Mrs. Kay stamps the inside and pushes it back across the desk to Birdie.

"Red," Birdie says with a big smile.

"You know, Birdie, you can take out more than one book. There are new books on the table there." Mrs. Kay points to the children's area, the way she does every week, even though we all know Birdie only wants one book and she wants to climb the ladder to get it. For the first time, it occurs to me that there's always a red book sticking out from a shelf that's low enough for Birdie to see but still high enough to climb to.

"Big red," Birdie says.

Then she points to the calendar on Mrs. Kay's desk. It's the kind where you tear off each day when it's done.

"Two candle," Birdie says.

"Yes!" I say. Birdie is right. The calendar says 2-4-2002, and Birdie had a wax candle in the shape of a 2 on her last birthday cake.

I find my books on the second shelf down from the ceiling. I don't think Mrs. Kay is surprised to see the titles, because she nods at the books, then nods at me, the son of Harlan Bower, part owner of Bower Brothers Northern Maine Well-Drilling Service.

"I hope they serve you well, Henry BOWER." She says my last name louder than my first, as if I need a reminder that I come from the well-drilling, dowsing Bower family.

"Thank you," I say. I like Mrs. Kay and I like that she's a librarian whose name is also a letter of the alphabet.

"You're welcome. You probably know your grandfather dowsed and drilled the town well for this library and the school and most of Main Street."

"I do. Were you there when the well was drilled?" I ask Mrs. Kay.

"Yes, I was. They hit a gusher at fifty feet."

"Did you hear anything?"

"The drilling rig is loud, of course. And everyone cheered when they hit water."

"I mean, did you hear anything when my grandfather was dowsing? Or see anything different? Or smell anything funny?"

Our neighbors in Lowington say my grandfather and my father and Lincoln call to the water and it answers back. I've never heard them call, unless it was words spoken so low I couldn't hear them.

"I don't believe I did, Henry, but I wasn't paying that

much attention. I know your grandfather cut an apple branch to dowse with from a tree out in back of the library. Maybe these books here"—Mrs. Kay points to the books I'm holding—"will help you."

"I hope so," I say.

"You know, I tell folks the homeschooled boy in Lowington takes more books out of the library than anyone else."

"You count them?" I ask her, surprised.

"I don't have to. You're my best customer."

She reaches under the desk and puts a rock down in front of me, the way she does every week that I come to the library.

I look closely. I pick it up and feel its weight in my hand, and I bring it to my nose to smell if there's any hint of the dirt it came from. It's an easy one.

"Milky quartz," I say. "Where did you find it?"

Mrs. Kay looks a little embarrassed.

"Right in my driveway. The plow truck kicked up some rocks."

If I'd had the chance to name it, I would have called it cloudy quartz because the color of the rock reminds me of the clouds that fill the sky before it rains.

"I never asked you before, Henry. Do you have a favorite kind of rock?"

"I like rocks with mica in them, and rocks with quartz stripes. Rectangular rocks are good for building stone walls. And I like the big glacial erratics in Braggy's woods. Dad says the glacier left them."

"It sounds like you never met a rock you didn't like! Remember, Henry," Mrs. Kay says, "when the snow finally melts, I want to stop by and see how your stone wall is coming along."

Birdie and I carry our books outside and look for Mom. She's across the street past Mr. Ronnie's Picker Palace, her cloth collecting bag over her shoulder. A long braid hangs down her back, tied at the end with a piece of Birdie's kite string. Mom's hair is the same color as the red fox we see at the edge of the field. Her pants are tucked into her winter boots. Mr. Ronnie stands in the doorway of his store, watching her with a frown on his face. He's a big man with more white than black in his mustache and short beard.

"One man's trash is another man's treasure. Or should I say, one WOMAN's trash is another man's treasure." Mr. Ronnie shakes his finger at Mom.

Does he think Mom is finding better things along the road than the ones he has in the Picker Palace? I've been in his store and it's so crowded I don't think he'd have room for much more. Mom and I sell the things we find on a card table at the bottom of our driveway, but it's not like Mr. Ronnie's secondhand store. We don't tell people what to pay. They take what they want and put whatever money they think it's worth in the wooden Honor Box.

Mom knows the wet places in the woods where fiddle-heads grow and sells them on the table in the spring. I put special rocks out for sale. Rocks that are smooth as duck eggs or shaped like hearts are good sellers. And one summer visitor told me she would buy as many flat rocks as I could find but they had to be at least a foot wide.

"Me and my son have a business to run, you know," Mr. Ronnie grumbles, loud enough so I can hear it in front of the library.

Mom stops and looks back at him, like he's speaking a language she doesn't know. Then she waves and smiles at him. "Hi there, Mr. Ronnie, nice day," she says.

Mr. Ronnie looks puzzled, as if now he can't understand what she's saying. He shakes his head and goes into the Picker Palace. The door slams behind him.

I hold Birdie's hand and we cross the road to see what's in the bag. "What did you find? Anything good for the table?"

Mom holds the bag open. There's a long bolt with a washer and a nut on the end. It has hardly any rust on it.

"It was lying on top of the snowbank," Mom says.

"I wonder what it came off," I say.

"Big red," Birdie tells Mom, hugging her book with both arms.

"Two books. Second-to-top shelf." I show Mom my books.

"Hizzz hizzzz." Birdie looks up at the winter sky.

"Is there a bird up there?" I ask her. Sometimes Birdie hears birds before we see them.

"No. *Hizzz*," she repeats, but I don't see anything.

When I'm ready for bed that night, I take my home-school notebook and a pencil out of my nightstand drawer. Every year on my birthday Mom gives me a new notebook with my name and age written on the front in black marker.

How do animals find watering holes? Do they see the reflection of the water in the sky or do they smell it from miles away?
Can you train your nose to smell water the way dogs learn to track people's scents?
What makes the dowsing stick move to the water?

My room is right across from the kitchen. I hear the thuds of my father stoking the stove with heavy chunks of firewood. The bang of the damper when he closes down the stove. The running of water in the kitchen. This last sound gets me out of bed.

I realize every night my father pours himself a glass of water, drinks it, then pours another and carries it down to his and Mom's bedroom. A grown man's body is sixty percent water. I wonder, if you drink more water, does the percent increase? If you have more water in your body, does it help you dowse?

When the kitchen is empty, I go in and run myself a glass of water and drink it. Then I pour myself another glass of water and set it on my nightstand next to my pillow. I bring my nose right to the edge of the glass and sniff, but I don't smell anything.

I fall asleep thinking about the water that feeds our wells on the hill. The top of Bower Hill Road is the highest point in town, and the house at the top is Nana's.

The next house down from Nana's is Uncle Lincoln's, my father's older brother. Lincoln has never wanted to live anywhere but here on the hill where he was born. He's pretty quiet, but if a neighbor has trouble, Lincoln is the first person they go to for help. The tall house down from that is Uncle Braggy's, the middle brother.

After Braggy's house there's a hedgerow of trees and then our big field. The fourth and last Bower house is ours. If you drive back up to the top of the hill and go down the other side, you pass the Bower gravel pit, granite quarry, and cemetery. Braggy's wife is buried in the family cemetery. Braggy's stone is next to hers, with his name and birth date already carved on it. If you keep going, you get to Bog Road. James and his father, Wendell, live on Bog Road.

Bower One, Bower Two, Bower Three, and Bower Four, I think of them, with our house and land being Bower Four. Past our house, at the bottom of the hill, where the road takes a curve toward town, are Bower Five and

Bower Six, the land and fields for my house and Birdie's when we grow up.

And under all of them, enough water that none of our wells have ever gone dry.

Suddenly, as if a voice is calling to me, I'm woken by a rustling and hissing noise.

Hizzz. Hizzzz.

It's like the sound Birdie made when she pointed toward the sky outside the library, and I remember the way the dowsing stick pointed upward instead of down.

I open my bedroom window, which faces the field.

HIZZZ. HIZZZZ.

I'm in my boots and out the front door. It's very cold and still, no wind blowing in my face. The sky is full of shooting stars and they're brighter than any I've ever seen before, but the hemlock trees around the house block part of my view.

I notice Dad's extension ladder leaning against the roof, for when he needs to break up ice dams or clean the chimney. It's an easy climb onto the roof of the house. I stand on the ridgepole, as high off the ground as I've ever been. I can see in every direction. The crackling gets louder and louder and there's a huge boom. Suddenly an explosion of light fills the whole sky overhead, and a dark shape arcs down onto the top of the field.

Then, except for the moon, the sky is dark. I blink once, twice, and it's still there—a shadow on the frozen white.

My hands sting from the cold and I scramble down the roof and back into the house. I open the damper on the stove, throw in a stick of kindling and a bigger piece of wood, and rub my hands together as the fire heats up.

I know scientists aren't sure if there's an end to the universe. I read that you can travel at the speed of light forever without reaching an edge of it. But when I was balanced on top of the roof watching the light burst over me, it felt real, how big the universe is.

"Henry?" Mom comes into the hallway in her long winter nightgown. Did she hear the front door open or close? "Are you feeling okay?"

"Yes, I just put more wood in the stove."

She points to the crescent of moon in the kitchen window.

"It's waning."

This is when I could say what I saw in the sky and what I think crashed onto the field. Mom would find Dad's headlamp and go outside with me.

But I don't want to say anything until I find out for sure myself.

"See if you can go back to sleep. It's still dark out." She yawns.

"I will."

Mom says darkness comes for a reason—to show us when to rest. I go into my room, but I can't sleep.

There's a picture I remember from my M encyclopedia.

I turn to the page that shows a meteor bursting through the atmosphere on its way down to Earth. It looks just like the explosion of light I saw from the roof.

Underneath, it says:

Meteors rarely blaze for more than a few seconds.
Meteors that reach Earth before burning up are meteorites.

Meteorites are rocks from space, the rarest rocks, and I've never seen or touched one in my whole life.

CHAPTER FOUR

When a fireball suddenly appears (and there's
never any warning) it is such an astonishing
moment that most people are spellbound.
—O. Richard Norton, *Rocks from Space*

BIRDIE COMES INTO my room and wakes me
up, pulling her red sled behind her. In her other hand she
holds her yellow stuffed duck, Lilygirl. At night Birdie
sleeps with Lilygirl on her crib mattress in Mom and
Dad's room down the hall.

"Mama sleep," Birdie tells me. "Dad sleep."

Maybe what fell from the sky came to Birdie, who cares
more than the rest of us what's up there past the weather
vane spinning in the wind. Birdie gets her name from the
first words she spoke. "Me Birdie," she said, pointing at a
flock of geese flying south before winter. Their honking
was loud and sad at the same time.

I've been alive for one hundred percent of Birdie's
life, and she's only been alive for twenty percent of mine,
but I feel like there was never a time I didn't know her.

I'm always doing the math in my head. When I'm
twenty, Birdie will be twelve. When I'm fifty, Birdie
will be forty-two. The longer we both live, the greater

the percent of my life I'll have known her. When I'm ninety-nine and Birdie is ninety-one, I'll have known her ninety-one-point-nine-one percent of my life.

Sometimes I think Birdie is lucky because she has eight more years where she doesn't have to worry about being a dowser or not. She can just play with Lilygirl and sled and watch for birds and swing on Nana's swing.

"Mom and Dad will be awake soon. Want to go see something in the field?" I ask her.

"Slide down," Birdie says.

"Sure. But I want to show you something first."

Birdie puts Lilygirl in her high chair.

"Be good," she tells her.

I get dressed and help Birdie into her coat and boots. Her winter coat is as red as a cardinal's and she rides on my back, my arms circling her skinny legs as I tromp toward the place where the dark shape came to rest during the night.

We walk past the garden covered in snow and ice, past the empty clothesline, past the blackberry patch into the wide, sloping field that goes from the old stone wall bordering it at the top down sharply to the road. The same field where James found the antler and Birdie sledded.

Something in the top corner of the field, below the hedgerow between our land and Braggy's, looks like a giant boulder. It's twice as tall as I am and wider on the bottom than on its flat top. It's black and in the sun its surface shines like colored glass.

I stand still, staring at the rock that's so big I can't see past it. I remember the way my dowsing stick pulled upward yesterday. Did the rock also come to me? Before I fell asleep last night, I read more about meteors and meteorites. I hoped the shadow I saw on the snow would be a space rock, maybe the size of the ones in my stone wall. I imagined picking it up and studying it. I didn't imagine anything this size!

"GO, Henry." Birdie wiggles her legs up and down.

There's a shallow crater around the rock that makes it look like a giant upside-down teacup sitting in a huge egg-shaped saucer. Outside the crater is a jagged circle of melted snow, and the blades of grass near it are bright green. Even though it's so cold out my face stings, the snow outside the crater is slushy under my boots.

"Hat," Birdie chirps in my right ear. "Hat, hat, hat."

The rock does have the shape of a hat—an enormous shiny-looking hat. As we get closer, I see that the surface is not as smooth as it looked from a distance. It has indentations on it that look like thumbprints. There are also specks of something as silver as the blade of my father's sharpened axe.

"Touch." Birdie pokes my chin. "Touch hat."

When I don't move, she pokes me harder.

My father's nickname for Birdie is the Boss. "What does the Boss think about that?" he'll ask Birdie. If there aren't any people around to boss, Birdie tries to catch the dragonflies that crisscross the yard in the summer, or she calls to the big green luna moths to land on her finger.

"TOUCH!" Birdie shouts in my right ear. I let her down and we approach the giant boulder together.

I kneel down in the hollow that is the crater and touch the rock where it meets the ground. It's very hard. I try to scrape off the shiny metal specks with a fingernail, but nothing happens. I press my thumbs into the rounded pits and run my hands down the ridges that can't be smoothed out and the creases that can't be straightened.

Careful not to let Birdie see, I lick it with the tip of my tongue. It has no taste I recognize. Maybe ashes, maybe very old wood. The metal is smooth, with a warmth that surprises me on this very cold day.

There's a smell that comes to me from down there at the bottom of the rock. I've smelled it every year for ten years. Spring. But this time it's two months early.

Birdie has both hands on the rock, as high up as she can reach. She pushes. Then pushes harder.

She backs up to where the hard-packed winter snow meets the new slush in the crater and runs at the rock with her arms out. There's not even the tiniest bit of movement. It's as if the rock has grown roots or legs that are locked into the earth. It won't topple over the way people do when she runs at them.

Birdie changes tactics and reaches her arms as far as she can in both directions and gives its hard, blocky surface a hug. She lays her head on the big boulder and looks up toward the sky.

I crawl around the rock on my hands and knees, soaking my jeans. All the sides are the same bluish black, but some have more silvery veins, and some are more dimpled than others. I wish I had seen the bottom of the rock before it landed. Is it the same color? Is it bumpy or smooth? I'm also curious how far the bottom of the rock sank into the earth.

Birdie presses herself against the big glassy rock. The melted snow in the crater almost reaches the tops of her red rubber boots now. Maybe the Boss, always looking above, recognizes the rock, because she acts like they're already friends.

I want to say something to the big rock myself, to welcome it the way my parents make visitors, even strangers, feel at home. Then I remember what my mother says when she finds a mushroom or fern she can't identify.

"I don't know your name, but I'm glad to meet you," I say to the big rock.

"Name BIRDIE." Birdie laughs.

I laugh, too, when she says that.

"I meant the rock, not *you*, Birdie. I know *your* name."

My hand rests on the hard surface of the stone. I breathe in the spring smell. And I think about my trip to the museum and what happened to the twelve-thousand-year-old woolly mammoth tusk. If you can even call something a tusk if it doesn't have one single particle of the real tusk in it.

I press one finger to my lips. "The rock here. This is our secret. Can you say 'I'll keep the secret, Henry'?"

"Tell James," Birdie says.

"Okay, we'll show James when he gets out of school. Won't he be excited when he sees it? But don't tell anyone else."

Birdie reaches out and puts her finger on my lips the way I did.

"Big hat," she says.

Birdie is shivering, and my legs are cold in my wet jeans. I'm suddenly hungry for the breakfast I forgot to have.

"Let's get home where it's warm and dry off and have something to eat," I tell her.

On the walk home, I think about how old the stone might be and if it was traveling toward us when Bower Hill Road was still covered by a glacier.

The mammoth lived during the Ice Age. Nana watched Birdie while my mother took me and James to the Maine State Museum to see the tusk for my tenth birthday last year. It was a very long drive, two hundred and forty-five miles south, which is seventy-five percent of the whole length of Maine and thirty percent farther than anywhere else I'd ever been.

After Mom paid for us to get in, I hurried past the

displays about sardine packing and ice harvesting straight to the mammoth exhibit. But when I got there, the sign underneath the tusk said:

REPLICA

The volunteer at the museum explained that when the tusk was tested to see how old it was, and to make a mold of it, it was destroyed in the process. He said the replica was even more accurate than the original one had been. He pointed to a mammoth tooth that *was* real.

The tooth and the replica both hung on a wall behind glass. I got as close to the glass as I could, but there was no way to tell by looking what the tooth felt or smelled like. And I knew the replica wouldn't have the muddy smell from the pond where the real tusk was found.

The volunteer was very proud of the replica. I thanked him for explaining about the tusk and told him how far we'd come to see it.

James liked seeing the replica and the tooth. He loved the steam locomotive, the three-story waterwheel, and the stuffed seabirds on the pretend beach. Mom spent a long time looking at the hull fragment from a wooden ship that ran aground after a midnight collision with another boat. The fragment was bigger than my uncle Lincoln's whole house.

On our way out, we got postcards at the museum gift

shop. I picked one that showed the real tusk in the ground where it was found. During the long drive home, I studied the postcard of the tusk they'd used to make the replica and thought about the real mammoth tooth, which was bigger than my head.

I didn't know then that I'd get to see and touch something much, much older than the tusk. A rock in our hayfield that could be even older than the sun.

CHAPTER FIVE

*The Inuits revealed to Robert E. Peary,
the famous American explorer,
the locations of three of the meteorites.
The Inuits called the masses
Ahnighito or Tent (31 tons),
Woman (3 tons) and Dog (0.4 tons).*
—ALEX BEVAN AND JOHN DE LAETER,
METEORITES: A JOURNEY THROUGH SPACE AND TIME

I WAIT FOR JAMES to come on the school bus. When his father, Wendell, works the evening shift at the paper mill, James stays with us. Birdie is visiting Nana up at Bower One.

James goes to the brick school on Main Street in Lowington. I've never ridden the yellow school bus that passes me and Mom on our walks. It barrels past our house, collecting all the children in Lowington except me.

Once when I was little and Mom and I were in the supermarket, Mrs. Stockford from Bog Road peered down at me and asked, "Now, why aren't YOU in school, little man?"

I shrugged. I didn't know what to say. When we got

home I asked Mom if she forgot I was supposed to go to school.

"No," she said, kneeling down to look me in the eye, "you can learn whatever you want right here at home. What do you want to study?"

The answer came to me all by itself. "I want to break open rocks and see what's inside. And I want to dig holes."

So Mom found me plastic goggles and a sledgehammer. The sledgehammer was heavy, but it wasn't long before I could lift the hammer and split a rock open in one blow. Dad gave me a short shovel and let me dig in the front yard. Deep down in my holes I found dirt-covered rocks, spotted newts, salamanders, and bits of clay.

Every year after that, when fall came, Mom asked me, "Home or school?" I didn't know if there was a right or wrong answer. This year it was close. Maybe fifty-five percent home and forty-five percent school. But there could only be one answer.

While I wait for James, I look in the M and the R volumes, reading about the biggest rocks that fell to Earth. Braggy got the set of red-and-black encyclopedias at a farm auction when I was six. He bid on a box of carpentry tools and in the bottom under the tools were the encyclopedias.

"You read these, Henry," Braggy said, laughing, when he gave them to me, "and you'll know everything there is to know. Then you can tell ME."

I knew he was joking, but I wondered if maybe it was true.

What I find in the encyclopedias makes me worried. One gigantic meteorite was loaded onto a boat, sailed across an ocean, and put in a museum. Another was secretly dragged through the woods on a homemade wagon so the man could claim it fell on his land. Pieces of the biggest meteorite in the world were cut off by people to make metal tools out of the iron rock. I learn that no matter how big or special a meteorite is, someone always wants to take it or chip it.

When I hear the bus coming down the hill, I run out to meet James.

"How was school?" I ask him.

"Good. How was home?"

"VERY good. I have something to show you up in the field. A secret."

"You found a mammoth tusk up there?" James guesses.

"No."

"The other antler?"

"No, no tusks or antlers."

I lead the way up the hill as fast as I can. The icy crust is gone and the snow is soft. James is good at keeping secrets. He didn't tell anyone about the groundhog hole we found near Braggy's shed last summer. We both liked the long tunnels the groundhog dug with no tools but its body, even if it chewed Mom's sunflower seedlings down to their roots.

"Hey, my sneakers are all wet." James lifts his foot to show me.

"Sorry about that," I say. "Do you want to wear my boots?"

"That's okay. The snow's not mushy like this around our trailer."

The R encyclopedia didn't have anything about a rock that melts snow or turns grass green in the winter.

"You can dry your sneakers by the stove when we get back," I say.

"What is that giant THING?" James shouts when the big rock comes into sight. "It's HUGE! Where did it come from? Did it roll down from the top of the hill? Did you find it by dowsing?"

"It came from the sky," I say.

"How do you know that?" James turns to me.

"I saw it fall."

The crater is filled with water now. The heavy meteorite looks like it's floating in a swamp of its own creation. The winds gusting around the rock are blowing warm air instead of cold.

James walks around the meteorite the way I did the first time.

"Wow! I never saw a rock like this. Not even in Braggy's gravel pit. You found the best thing ever!"

"I saw a picture of a really big meteorite called the Ahnighito in the M encyclopedia," I tell James. "It fell in Greenland and it has a shape sort of like this one. The people who lived there called it the Tent."

"It does look kind of like a tent. Maybe you could go see that one sometime."

"It's not in Greenland anymore," I explain. "In the M encyclopedia it says when Admiral Peary found out about it, he moved it across the ice and into a boat, sailed it across the ocean, and sold it to the American Museum of Natural History in New York City for forty thousand dollars."

"Forty thousand dollars! For a rock. No wonder you want to keep it a secret," James says.

That's not why I want to keep it secret.

I don't want it taken from the place where it fell.

I don't want it chipped or cut.

I didn't read anything about a meteorite being made into a replica, but I wouldn't want that to happen, either.

But I know I can't keep it secret for long.

Even if Birdie doesn't tell, in the spring Mom goes into the woods to put out taps and buckets for maple sugaring. Her path to the woods goes right by the rock.

In the summer, Dad hays the field in a neat square, but now there's a big rock in the corner of it. What if the field is too wet to drive on when the grass is ready to cut and the tractor gets stuck?

Since it fell, my thoughts are ninety percent about the big rock. Everything else is squeezed into the remaining ten percent. It feels like the rock—and me—are waiting for something to happen, but I don't know what that something is.

CHAPTER SIX

The first meteorite fall for which written records
exist is the Ensisheim meteorite, which fell on the
village of Ensisheim (now in the Alsace region of
France) in 1492. A large fireball was observed and,
after a large explosion . . . caused much fright and
excitement amongst the local people.
—Caroline Smith, Sara Russell,
and Gretchen Benedix, *Meteorites*

AT BREAKFAST the next morning, my father flips
ployes, the buckwheat pancakes we all love, on the hot
cast-iron griddle. Birdie sits in her high chair with Lilygirl.

"Eat, Lilygirl." Birdie holds the duck under one arm
and offers her a piece of a ploye.

Uncle Braggy comes to the door and sticks his head in.

"The wind blew the smell of coffee and ployes into
my bedroom window and woke me right up," Braggy tells
us, coming in and settling himself down at the table next
to me. My father puts out an extra plate and fork for him.
Braggy has black hair like my father and Uncle Lincoln
and me, but his is curly instead of straight, and when he
stands next to his tall brothers, the top of his head only
comes up to their shoulders.

"I think the wind blows *down* the hill, not up, Braggy,"
I say.

"The wind out there's blowing every which way this
morning, Henry. If it gets any stronger, I might have to tie
myself down! But I didn't just come for breakfast. I want
to show you what's in the paper today."

"Is there a new winner of the Boston Post Cane?" I
ask him. The oldest person in town gets a real ebony-and-
gold cane. Braggy wants to be the oldest person in town
one day and be presented with the cane at a special cer-
emony and get his picture in the paper.

"No, it's still Isadora True. One hundred and one. But
look at this!"

Braggy holds up the newspaper and I read the word
in big letters:

FIREBALL

"There was a bright streak of light seen over this part
of northern Maine night before last. A space rock broke
up in the air," Braggy announces.

I drop my fork on the floor. Mom pours maple syrup
on Birdie's ployes and passes the jar to me. Dad watches
the ployes cook with his spatula ready. I'm thinking this
would be the time to say what I saw—to tell my family
about the stone, to share the secret. Then Braggy holds
up the paper again.

"A collector is offering a reward to anyone who finds a
piece of it. They're paying a thousand dollars. For a piece

as big as that dinner plate." Braggy points to the plate of ployes in the middle of the table. "I'm also guessing whoever finds it is gonna get their picture on the front page of the paper."

"A thousand dollars? What would you do with a thousand dollars, Braggy?" Dad asks him.

"I'd buy myself a windmill so I could make my own electricity when the wind blows. They have ones so tall they'd catch the wind going down *and* up the hill. I'd rig a pulley from the woodshed to the house so all I'd have to do is press a button and my firewood would be delivered right to the stove."

"Don't go counting that money yet, Braggy. Northern Maine is a big place," my father says. "Finding a piece of rock that size would be like finding a needle in a haystack. Pieces could have fallen deep in the woods."

"Or in the river," Mom adds.

"I know that, and I have a plan," Braggy tells us. "I'm going to drive up and down the roads after dark and look for something that glows."

"I'm not sure rocks from space glow in the dark, Braggy. They're bright when they come through into the atmosphere because they get heated up," I say, then add, because he looks so excited about his plan, "but if they did glow, that would be a great idea."

"What would *you* do with the reward money?" I ask my mother.

"I don't know, Henry. We could use some of it to take a trip down to Boston to see the big science museum there."

"What would *you* do with the reward?" I ask my father.

"Guess I'd save it for a rainy day," my father answers.

"That's right," Braggy says, laughing, "and if you forgot your umbrella, you could go out and buy one for every day of the year!"

"Speaking of winds and the weather," my father says, "have you noticed what's happening out in the hayfield?"

Uh-oh, I think.

My father stretches his head toward the kitchen window, where you can see a small part of the field. Only my room off the kitchen has a full view.

"What's happening?" I hold my breath, waiting for his answer.

"Nearly all the snow is gone off the hayfield just about overnight. Never seen it this early."

I let my breath out. It doesn't surprise me that my father is the first one to notice something unusual happening in the field. Does his forked stick of apple wood or do his dowsing hands let him know there's a shift in the underground water on Bower Hill Road?

"Could be the culvert is clogged up with leaves, not letting the field drain," Mom suggests.

Culverts, the corrugated steel tubes set under roads

and driveways all through town, direct the rain and melt-ing snow away from places where people need to walk and drive. Mom and I find cans and bottles and people's lost mittens in the culverts. I used to crawl in the culverts, but now I'm too big to do that, so I use a stick to drag out what I can't reach.

"Still very early for snowmelt," Dad says again.

"Big hat," Birdie says, spreading her arms wide, her fingers sticky with maple syrup. One hand holds Lilygirl.

"Birdie!" I turn my chair to look Birdie right in the eyes, staring hard to get her attention and remind her, without words, about our secret. Especially now that I know about the reward.

Birdie's mossy eyes are more green than brown when she laughs. She looks right back at me, and I can't tell if it means she will keep the secret or tell it.

My father takes off his brim hat and sets it on Birdie's head.

"Big enough for you, Boss?" He laughs and gets up from the table.

"Touch hat," Birdie says.

"Go right ahead," my father says on his way outside.

I'm glad Birdie only says two words at once, but I realize it's just a matter of time before my father goes out in the field to investigate why spring has come to Bower Four before anywhere else in town.

Braggy takes the last ploye with his fingers and uses it to wipe up the rest of the maple syrup on his plate.

"Braggy," I ask him, "are you thirsty? Do you want a glass of water?"

"I haven't finished my coffee yet." He holds up his mug.

"Do you like water? Dad drinks a glass of water every night before he goes to bed. Do you?"

"Sure, Henry, I LOVE water—especially for putting out fires." Braggy thumps his leg and laughs at his own joke.

Another answer that's not exactly an answer. Though Braggy's jokes make everyone laugh.

I pick up the newspaper Braggy brought and read the article about the reward. Everything he told us is true.

One thousand dollars for a small piece of the fireball that landed in Northern Maine.

If someone would pay that much money for a piece the size of a plate, what would the big rock up in the field be worth?

A museum paid forty thousand dollars for the Ahnighito meteorite.

More money than me and Mom could ever make at the yard sale table.

CHAPTER SEVEN

Meteorites are naturally of the greatest scientific interest and value since they are the only samples of material from beyond the Earth-Moon System which can be studied and analyzed in the laboratory.

—ROBERT BURNHAM, JR.,
BURNHAM'S CELESTIAL HANDBOOK

LATER IN THE DAY, when Birdie is up at Bower One with Nana, I visit the meteorite by myself.

"Okay if I sit on you?" I ask.

The surface ridges and thumbprints make it easy to get a toehold in the glassy outer crust and climb up. I sit on the flat top of the giant stone and write in my homeschool notebook.

Where did you come from?
Why did you leave?
Do you miss the place you came from?
Was it dark where you were or were there stars to light up the sky?
Was it ice-cold or was it so hot that it melted your metal?
Was it noisy or quiet?

Did you break off from a bigger rock?
How old are you?
Why are you melting the snow?

It's like sitting on a rock island with a moat around it.

Did you ever see a bigger sun than our sun?
Did you steer yourself to land here or was it
by accident?
How far into the ground are you?
If my father tried to drill through you,
would you break?
Or would the drill break?

The meteorite is the new sun in my universe, the very center of everything, and I'm like its Earth.

If the rest of my family were planets, Birdie would be Mercury, the smallest planet, and Mom would be Venus, the second planet, shrouded in clouds. Dad would be Mars, the fourth and only planet besides Earth with liquid water on its surface. James would be the moon, Earth's closest companion. Even if Earth and the moon are traveling at different speeds, they always keep each other in sight.

Braggy would want to be Jupiter, the biggest planet. I feel bad that he's going to drive around looking for a glow-in-the-dark rock, when the big stone is right here in our field.

The snow is all gone from the field, and the ground is soggy. When I get back to the house, I hang my socks and jeans on the drying rack in front of the wood stove. Even my body is damp, and my feet smell like Nana's dirt floor cellar after a rain.

While my clothes dry, I sit barefoot at the kitchen table in my pajama pants, looking at the M volume of *The World Book Encyclopedia*. I read about the biggest meteorite discovery ever—the sixty-six-ton Hoba meteorite that fell in Africa. It was discovered by a farmer when he was plowing his field with an ox.

A car honks outside, and one, two, then three cars pull into our driveway. It's more cars than ever stopped at the same time on our road.

"Wow! Table rush! Three cars at once," I call out to Mom, who's planting tomato seeds in cardboard egg cartons. "I'll go see what they want."

The things we have on the yard sale table now are a striped scarf, a clay flowerpot, a metal rake, an old map, and two heart-shaped rocks.

Once in a while people have a twenty-dollar bill and want change, like the table is the town store. One time a man wanted to know how much for EVERYTHING on the table, and the TABLE, too. Mom says you can learn a lot about people by the way they react to the Honor Box.

The cars all start honking. One after the other.

HONK HONK HONNNNKKK

I rush to pull my wet jeans over my pajama pants, step barefoot into my boots, and run out the door.

There are five cars now—parked every which way in the driveway and along the road. Some people left their engines running and doors open, as if they were in too big a hurry to turn off their cars and close their doors. Most of the people are running down the road.

"What's going on?" I call out. "Is there a moose blocking the way?"

"The road's flooded."

"Road's impassable."

"Looks like a river down there."

"Your daddy drill for water in the middle of the road, did he?" Mr. Stockford asks me. He walks slowly, a cane in one hand. Mrs. Stockford holds his other arm.

"No, sir, he did not," I answer.

"I hear Harlan is going to repaint the sign on his drilling rig to say Bower Brothers *and Son*," Mr. Stockford says.

My breath catches in my throat. Could it be true? Dad is so sure I'm a dowser that he's repainting the sign?

"He said he was going to do that?"

Mr. Stockford pats the top of my head lightly and laughs.

"I'm just kidding you, but you sure look just like your grandfather when he was young. Are you going to be a dowser, too?"

No matter how many times I'm asked that question, I'm not sure what the right answer is. Did Braggy get asked that, too, when he was my age?

"I don't know. I'd like to be a dowser," I find myself saying.

This is the first time I've said this to anyone. I'm surprised it makes me feel good instead of bad to say it.

"People are always going to need water," Mr. Stockford says, as if my answer was just what he wanted to hear.

"Speaking of water, do you folks have a boat?" Mrs. Stockford asks me.

"No, we don't," I say. "A boat? Why would we need a boat?"

"You're gonna need one if you intend to go down that way."

"Oh no," I say. "It can't be that bad."

"Come take a look. We saw it when we came over the hill." Mrs. Stockford shakes her head. "It's *that* bad."

I follow her onto the road. I hear the water before I see it. It isn't the rapids of the Saint John River or ocean waves crashing on the rocky coast. This is a quieter, steadier noise that sounds like rain.

Down from Bower Four, past where the people are standing, is the land for my house when I'm older, the field below the field where the big rock sits. Bower Five, which I will now need a boat to reach.

When we get closer, I see that the road past our house is gone. Churning water courses down our sliding hill and across the road in a stream so wide I can't even see where it ends. It's water unlike any I've seen before. Not muddy at all, it runs a clear blue, but there are also swirling currents of green and yellow.

"Stand back, kids," a woman who lives across from James warns some small children who walk toward the water.

"We don't know how deep it is."

"Or how fast it's running."

"Weird color."

"Is it blue or green? Or maybe yellow?"

"Strange."

"Isn't this all Bower land out here?" Mr. Ronnie's son, Dwayne, points up the hill, then down the hill, saying the two words together. Bowerland. The way he says it makes Bowerland sound like a bad thing. He wears wire-rimmed glasses like Mr. Ronnie, and a big dog with short black-and-white hair sits by his side. When he waves his hand in the air, the dog looks up.

"Always has been," Mrs. Stockford says.

"Shouldn't we call someone?"

"The sheriff should set up a barricade."

"It's going to break up the road," Perley Gaucher warns the crowd. He owns the town store on Main Street, and his daughter, Fiona, is in James's class. She once bought a heart-shaped rose quartz rock from the yard sale table, and I noticed that in the sun the freckles on her face looked like constellations.

"HAHA." I hear Uncle Braggy's voice. "And then the town will be buying *my* gravel and sand to fix it."

"Not exactly," Mr. Gaucher says. "The town will be after your baby brother for diverting his runoff onto a town road."

"Runoff! Something more than runoff is going on here."

"Where's it coming from?" a little girl asks, but no one seems to hear her.

If you knew where to look, you could see the hatlike shape of the meteorite up on the hill. Everyone is talking or pointing or shouting, but all I hear is the unstoppable movement of water coming from the place I saw the big rock land. I need to see it up close and put my hand in it, and I walk past the grown-ups to the edge of the water.

I kneel down and dip the tips of my fingers into the water and swish them around like I do in the bathtub. I put my fingers in my mouth. The water tastes like the big rock. Everything becomes quiet when my fingers are in the water, but when I take them out, the voices start up again behind me.

Mom walks down the road toward the crowd, and Dad and Nana come down the hill from Bower One. Dad carries Birdie in his arms.

All around me, the crowd talks.

"We should call someone."

"Who? The game warden?"

"Yes, it could be beavers. Maybe they flooded a stream uphill. They can do some real damage."

"Beavers the size of COWS." Braggy's voice is louder than everyone else's. "You can look for them from the roof of my house. It's the tallest house on the hill."

"Call the fire department," Mrs. Stockford suggests.

"The state police. They need to be informed."

"Yes, and maybe the department of transportation."

"How about the town manager?"

"Hahaha." Braggy snickers. "Call the coast guard. Call the US Navy. Call a lifeguard."

"That's enough, Braggy." My uncle Lincoln stands next to his younger brother. "These people have reason for concern. And so do we."

All of a sudden, Mom is there with me at the water. She lays her hands on top of my head. She takes a piece of my damp hair and moves it between her fingers, like she's trying to figure something out. I stand still, at the edge of the water. When I look away from the water up Bower Hill, I see the last curve of the sun lighting up the earth. It's only five-thirty but the sun goes down early in February. As it gets darker, I can't see the colors in the water anymore, but I hear it rushing past at my feet.

By the time it's completely dark, the state police have

set up floodlights and blocked off the road in both directions. Two police cars are parked at the bottom of our driveway. It's never been this bright outside at night since the fireball flashed across the field.

Birdie falls asleep in Dad's arms, and he lays her down on her mattress in his and Mom's room.

I pour myself a glass of water and drink it down. Then I pour another glass and set it on my nightstand. The blue lights on the police cars make strange, shifting patterns across my bedroom walls.

I'm fifty percent worrying and fifty percent excited about what it's going to look like out there when morning comes.

I open my window a hand's width so I can hear the sound of the rain that's not really rain. No one is saying what will happen if the blue moving water streaming over Bower Hill Road can't be stopped. When he drills a well, Dad always tells people you can never have too much water, but this water can't be controlled with a shutoff valve. So I worry that once the sun is up, we might see what too much water really looks like.

CHAPTER EIGHT

The larger the meteoroid, the brighter the meteor.
The brightest ones are known as fireballs.
—HEATHER COUPER AND NIGEL HENBEST,
SPACE ENCYCLOPEDIA

"HENRY, WAKE UP." James is standing by my bed. "It's crazy out there. There's a helicopter in Nana's yard. And it looks like a town meeting in your house. Here, your mom said to give you these."

He hands me a pile of folded clothes that are still warm from being next to the wood stove.

"The newspaper people are outside ready to interview your family, but your mom said they needed to wait for you."

"What time is it?"

"Seven-thirty. Our neighbors across the road told us about the flood this morning, and Dad let me ride my bike over. I can't believe how much water there is down there."

I put on the warm pants, socks, and flannel shirt. I'm still thirsty, but it's the first time in days I've felt dry.

"What's it doing?" I ask James.

"Still flooding the road. It's moving really fast."

All I remember hearing when I woke up during the night was the sound of the water through my window. I didn't even hear the helicopter land on top of Bower Hill.

It does look like a town meeting in the house. There are maps spread open on the kitchen table. The people crowded in the kitchen have shirts and jackets that say EMERGENCY MANAGEMENT and FOREST SERVICE and MAINE STATE POLICE. The town manager is there, too, and some of our neighbors. I smell coffee and something sweet.

"You slept well, Henry, even with all this commotion?" Mr. Emery, the town manager, asks me.

"Yes, I think the water put me to sleep," I say.

I look for my coat and hat. They're hanging by the wood stove, so they're warm, too. Before we go outside, I pull off one of the two round magnets holding Birdie's cloud drawing on the refrigerator. I center the remaining magnet so the picture hangs straight and put the other magnet in my front coat pocket.

Dad says news travels fast in a small town. The gathering outside is even bigger than yesterday. Big wet flakes of snow are coming down and sticking to people's coats and hats.

"This is my nephew, Henry," Braggy's booming voice says, announcing us, "and the blond boy behind him is James LaPlante. I taught both those boys how to throw the fastest fastball you ever saw."

The Channel 6 Northern Maine news crew has a

camera set up on the dry part of the road uphill from the flood.

"Let's get started now that all the Bowers are here." A young woman directs me to where she's lined up my father, holding Birdie, and my mother in front of the camera. The woman guides me so I'm standing next to my father.

James goes and stands next to Mom. She's the only mother he remembers.

"I'm almost a Bower," James tells the newswoman. "My father says I'm here more than I'm home. Birdie probably thinks I'm her brother, too. Right, Birdie?"

Birdie has a doughnut in each hand. Sprinkles in one hand, chocolate frosted in the other.

"Find ant," Birdie says, pointing to James with the hand holding the sprinkle doughnut.

"That's right, Birdie. I found the antler," James says.

Mom puts an arm around James's shoulders, bringing him closer to her, and the newswoman doesn't make him move.

I can hear the rushing of the water behind me, and all I want to do is go down there with James and look at the swirling colors.

"It's February seventh," the woman says into a microphone, "and we are here with the Bower family. They live on the land where there is an unexplained flood happening here in Lowington. In fact, a road is now a stream. Let me ask you, Mr. and Mrs. Bower, how shocked are you by this flooding on your land?"

"Shocked," Birdie says, starting in on her sprinkle doughnut.

"Can I say something?" I ask, and reach for the newswoman's microphone.

"All right." The woman looks surprised, but she gives me the microphone. "Sure, let's hear what young Henry Bower has to say about all of this."

I've never spoken to so many people at once or talked into a microphone before. When I start to speak, my voice is louder than I've ever heard it, echoing around my head. It almost seems like my voice is coming out of the microphone instead of my mouth, the microphone saying the words I hope will explain the secret.

"Every year thousands of meteorites land on Earth. Some come from the asteroid belt, some from Mars and the moon, and some, a very rare type, from comets. I'm not sure, but I think it's possible that a rock could come from a place no one knows about and have special powers. When a person actually sees a meteorite land, it's called a fall. And meteorites are finders keepers. If you find one on your land, it belongs to you."

"Hey there, can someone tell Rock Boy we have work to do here on Earth?" a man grumbles.

"ROCK BOY IS RIGHT!" Uncle Braggy shouts to the crowd. He is louder without a microphone than I am *with* one. "This boy knows more about building a stone wall than me, and that's saying a LOT. And he's been breaking rocks open with a sledgehammer since he was old enough to stand," Braggy adds, exaggerating the truth more than a little.

"I can verify that fact!" Mrs. Kay shouts from the back of the crowd. "Henry Bower is quite an expert when it comes to the identification of rocks and minerals. If he says it's a meteorite, I believe him."

"Very interesting facts, Henry." The newswoman looks annoyed and reaches for her microphone. "But maybe we can ask your parents about the flood now."

I gently pull the microphone back to my mouth.

"We HAD a fall. You know the article that was in the paper? About the reward for a piece of the meteor that was seen over Northern Maine? I saw the fireball from my bedroom window three nights ago. It fell right in our field and I think it's what's causing the flood."

I hand the microphone back to the newswoman.

The newswoman looks interested now instead of annoyed. She directs the camerawoman to start recording.

It's still snowing and cold enough that white puffs come out of people's mouths when they talk. Birdie gives me the chocolate-frosted doughnut, her second favorite, with a big smile. My parents stare at me, and Mom leans toward Dad and whispers in his ear. Mr. Ronnie edges closer to the front of the crowd. His green hat, which says

PICKER PALACE in black letters, is speckled with big flakes of snow, and they stick to his green-and-black-plaid wool coat. Snowflakes land on his wire-rimmed glasses and fog up the lenses.

"How big is this rock of yours?" he asks me.

I stretch my arms out wide.

"Big," I say.

"Big hat," Birdie says, and my father's eyebrows go up.

"You don't say, Boss?" my father says.

"It doesn't surprise me that my nephew found one of those glow-in-the-dark rocks. He's always got his eye out for things. But if you want to see a BIG rock"—Braggy tries to get Mr. Ronnie's attention—"I've got a rock as big as a TRACTOR in my woods. Probably been there since cavemen lived here."

"So where's this big rock of yours, son?" Mr. Ronnie ignores Braggy and comes right up to me.

"*I* can tell you that." Braggy is laughing before he even finishes his sentence. "Only a stone's throw away. HAHAHA."

James laughs loudly at Braggy's joke, and Mr. Ronnie cracks a tiny smile. The snow comes down harder from a white sky. Behind us, the snow falls into the moving water and disappears.

"Henry." James comes over to me. "Charge admission to see the rock. Just like in a museum. There's a lot of people here. I could collect the money for you. Like you said, you found it on your land. Finders keepers."

Instead of answering Mr. Ronnie or James, I do something I haven't done since I was Birdie's age. I close my eyes and hold my breath.

When I was little, I thought it would stop time.

I didn't know then that my heart kept beating and that the world outside my closed eyes continued moving.

I held my breath on the morning of my third birthday.

I held my breath the first time I saw the ocean.

Now I know that as I scrunch my eyes shut and hold the air in my throat, my feet are touching an Earth that turns on its axis at more than eight hundred miles an hour. That's faster than a 747 jet.

There's no on/off switch on the world like there is on my father's drilling rig.

If I close my eyes, the world doesn't disappear.

It's impossible to stop suns and planets that have been set in motion billions of years ago.

I can't turn back time and unsay what I said.

I can't pick up the secret I put down.

I'm getting dizzy. I can hold my breath much longer than when I was three.

I hear people talking.

"That child doesn't look well."

"He's the boy they keep at home."

"I heard he was a strange child."

"He's polite, but very quiet. Not like his uncle Braggy."

AR-OMPHH

All of a sudden the air is knocked out of my lungs,

and I'm lying on the ground. My eyes blink open. Birdie is sitting on my back. She must have launched herself out of Dad's arms straight at me. She looks happy that for the first time no one pretended to fall over for her.

Birdie's leap also knocks the doubt from my mind.

In its place is a new feeling. A deep pride in the meteorite.

For coming from so far away.

For melting the snow.

For bringing the water.

For showing the colors.

For gathering the crowd.

For making so much happen without moving an inch.

I get to my feet with Birdie on my back.

"I'll show you where it fell the night it lit up the sky," I tell the crowd.

CHAPTER NINE

Meteoritic metal responds to a magnet. If much
metal is present, the magnet will cling to the rock.
—John T. Wasson, Meteorites: Their Record
of Early Solar-System History

MY USUAL PATH to the big rock is more than
muddy now. My footprints fill up with water that's clear
blue with flashes of green and yellow. The soggy terrain
throws me off-balance. I expect it to be firm and yet it
shifts under me, as if there's an undertow moving below.
Birdie bounces herself on my back to match my lopsided
steps.

Mr. Ronnie comes up beside me and James and Birdie.

"I gotta see this rock for myself," he says. "Have you
folks put in for that reward yet?"

"No, we haven't. I'm not sure we will."

Mr. Ronnie says something, but I don't hear it because
just then the helicopter circles over us, round and round
and round. Its blades make more noise than my father's
drilling rig in full throttle.

"WAVING ME," Birdie shouts, pointing up at the helicopter. "WAVING ME."

Birdie is right. One person in the helicopter shakes

both hands back and forth in front of himself down toward the crowd. He doesn't look happy.

Birdie holds on to my neck with one arm and waves back up at the helicopter.

The helicopter circles a few more times and flies off downhill, following the direction of the flooded road.

The big rock lies in its swampy crater. The ground near it is spongy and the stream starts just below, gushing out of the ground in waves. It looks like someone turned on a huge faucet deep underground.

Mom walks around and around the rock, studying it from all sides. She touches it gently with the tips of her fingers.

"What a beautiful thing you are, come from so far away," she says to the meteorite.

"I've never seen rock like this." Dad runs his hand over the shiny black surface. "I wonder if the bottom of it broke through into the aquifer. The water below it is pumping out like a vein of water from a flowing artesian well. The rock might be made of some kind of metal. But these things"—my father puts a finger in the rough, grooved thumbprints the way I did—"look like some kind of stone."

The M encyclopedia tells what scientists find when they cut pieces off different meteorites and test them.

iron

nickel

magnetite
cobalt
carbon
olivine crystals
feldspar
black glass
trapped air
oxygen
extraterrestrial dust

Extraterrestrial dust means that some meteorites have dust in them from the beginnings of the earliest stars.

Stardust.

I already said out loud in the microphone what I needed to say about the stone, so I stand there watching everyone look at the big rock.

"Some people have all the luck," Mr. Ronnie says.

"Yeah, they're lucky it didn't fall on their house!"

"When you put it on the news, call it the Bower meteorite," James says to the newswoman, "'cause my friend Henry Bower found it on Bower Hill Road."

"I wonder what it weighs."

"It's really hard." A girl kicks at the stone and cries out, "Ow, it hurt me."

I don't like that she kicks the meteorite, but I don't want her to hurt herself, either.

"It would take a big excavator to move that thing."

"Or a crane."

"I don't think it's going anywhere soon."

"How can a rock cause a flood, even if it's from space?"

"It has a funny smell. I never heard of a rock that smelled."

"It smells like the inside of my greenhouse." A woman sniffs the big rock.

"I saw on TV that a meteorite caused the dinosaurs to go extinct. I'm gonna check on my pigs when I get home."

"How do you know it's a meteorite?" Priscilla, our town clerk, asks me. "Maybe you saw fireworks someone set off and came out here and found a rock. Plenty of big rocks around."

I take the round refrigerator magnet out of my coat pocket and hold it in my open hand. The magnet jumps out of my hand and sticks to the side of the stone.

"Whoa!" the camerawoman yells. "I didn't catch that on tape. Can you do it again?"

I'm as surprised as she is. Last night I read that most meteorites contain iron and that a magnet will stick to them. I wanted to test it on the big rock, but I didn't expect the magnet to fly out of my hand like that!

I'm reaching for the magnet when I sense that something is wrong. I haven't heard from Braggy since we reached the big rock. He isn't giving everyone his opinion about the flying magnet or the giant meteorite or Dad's artesian well theory. For once, there's not one word from him.

Braggy stands downhill from the meteorite, hands on his hips, staring silently out toward the gushing water. When I go down where he's standing, I see what the helicopter must have seen—water slowly spreading sideways in the direction of our house.

"I guess I'm smarter than I thought, building a three-story house," Braggy says, but he doesn't sound glad about it.

The helicopter circles back up the hill and a loudspeaker booms out,

"EVACUATION ORDER. EVACUATE TO HIGHER GROUND."

"Birdie, honey." Mom lifts Birdie into her arms. "We're going up to Nana's house. What do you want to take from home to Nana's?"

"Take ME."

"Yes, of course we'll take you. But what else?"

"Doughnuts," Birdie says, showing Mom the few doughnut crumbs left in her hand.

"Henry, James," Dad shouts to us over the sound of the helicopter, "this is the plan. We move as fast as we can to the back door of the house. You have ten minutes to take whatever you want that you can carry. And I do mean ten minutes. I wouldn't be surprised if the cellar is already flooding. Then we exit through the back door up to Nana's house."

"What about the meteorite?" I ask.

The big stone from the sky sits there unchanged and unbothered by the noise of the helicopter or the crowd. Snowflakes melt on its shiny black surface, and water continues tumbling down the hill below it.

"I don't think it's going anywhere," Dad says.

What I'm really asking is if I'll be able to get back to the meteorite again, but I'm not sure Dad can answer that question.

When we get to the house, I look around my room. What should I take in the ten minutes my father gave us? The glass of water I poured last night is still on my nightstand, and my bed is unmade because I left in a hurry this morning.

I drink the water in the glass. Then I pull my covers up on the bed and smooth them out. The only things that are not mine to lose are the book about dowsing and the book about water from the Lowington library. I put them in my backpack and add my homeschool notebook and pencil.

"Five minutes," my father calls out.

I open the top drawer of my dresser and stuff as many pairs of socks as I can fit in my backpack. Nana has a shelf on her cookstove that's good for rising bread and warming up socks.

I check my room again and grab one more thing—my pillow. Whenever my father comes back from an overnight trip to drill a well in another county, he always says there's nothing like putting your head on your own pillow at night.

James runs past my room. "I got Birdie's blanket," he calls out to me.

When James says that about Birdie's quilt, I remember Lilygirl. Birdie wasn't carrying her this morning. I hurry into Mom and Dad's room. Lilygirl isn't on Birdie's crib mattress. I run into the kitchen and she's not in Birdie's high chair. She's not in the living room, either.

"Two minutes," Dad hollers.

He's standing by the cellar door wearing his tool belt and holding Mom's egg carton of tomato seeds. I hear water trickling into the basement, and the big rock's smell fills the house.

"Dad. I looked all over and I can't find Lilygirl."

Dad hesitates a moment and looks quickly around the house. Lilygirl is nowhere to be seen.

"We can't wait. We need to go. It's time, James," he calls out.

James runs into the kitchen with a big black plastic bag. It's so heavy he's dragging it across the floor. Dad opens the back door for us to leave. He grips the metal doorknob for a few extra seconds before he closes it behind us.

CHAPTER TEN

Meteorites, and their parent planets, are the most likely sources of the Earth's water.
—ASTROBIOLOGY MAGAZINE

WHEN WE GET to the top of the hill, Birdie has the happiest face in Nana's house. She's in the living room swinging herself in the kid swing Nana had bolted to the rafters. Its chains and wooden seat hang almost to the floor so Birdie can get in and out of it herself. The house smells like the tapioca Nana is stirring on the cookstove.

Some of Nana's fingers are bent sideways and her knuckles are puffed up and red. She used to pull dandelions in the spring and can the greens the way her own mother did, but now it hurts her too much to do it. On the dresser in her room, Nana has a framed photo of her and her mother in the field next to the river where they picked dandelions. Once, I told Nana she looked the same in the picture as she did now and she kissed my cheek. It's true, though. Her hair is short and white instead of brown and long, but her face is the same, and she's not much taller than she was then.

"Nice swinging, Birdie," I say. I hold my backpack in one hand and my pillow in the other, not sure where to put them.

"Go high," she says, pumping her legs up and down, up and down.

James is the next-happiest person. He carefully sets down the heavy plastic bag in the middle of the living room rug.

"Guess what?" he says. "I brought something for everyone from the house. Isn't that great?"

I see exactly what Dad meant about James's one hundred percent. James has his head and arms practically inside the bag. The first thing he pulls out is for Mom.

"Here. For when you make ployes. I found it in your cupboard." He gives Mom a glass jar of her maple syrup.

"Thank you, James." She holds the jar carefully in two hands, as if the amber-colored syrup is liquid gold.

"This is for you." James shows Birdie her baby quilt. It's forty red and white squares all sewn together. Twenty red and twenty white. I know because I used to count them. It was my baby quilt Nana made before her fingers got too sore to sew. I gave it to Birdie when she was born. There are five long rows of eight squares. In the middle of each red square Nana sewed a white heart, and in the middle of the white squares there's a red heart.

"You funny," Birdie says, laughing to see him with her quilt.

"And look what else I remembered."

James reaches deep into the bag and brings out five toothbrushes, all different colors. The fifth one is the one Mom keeps for James when he stays overnight.

The next thing James takes out of the bag is small enough to fit in his hand. He gives it to Dad, who studies it carefully, as if he hasn't seen it before.

"Isn't that your father's compass?" Nana asks Dad.

"I saw it on your dresser and I remembered you said your father gave it to you," James explains to my father.

Dad looks like he wants to say something to James, but no words come out of his mouth.

Next, James takes out the wooden Honor Box with the slit on top to put money in.

Mom is sitting on the couch, and James puts it on her lap.

"We only had ten minutes. I snuck out the front door and ran down the driveway to get it for you."

Like Dad, Mom is silent as she stands and sets the Honor Box on the mantel over the fireplace.

"The last thing is for you, Henry," James says. "I saw it open on the couch and I thought you might want it."

James takes the M volume of *The World Book Encyclopedia* out of the bag.

"Thank you," I say, hugging the heavy book the same way Birdie hugs her big and red books from the library.

. . .

It's much later in the day, after supper, when the side door opens and Uncle Lincoln comes in. He has black hair like me, and his ears stick out from the sides of his head. I used to want ears like Lincoln's, because I thought they would give me special hearing powers. I wanted to hear grubs eating grass, voles tunneling under the snow, and sap running in the trees.

"Hi, Mom," Lincoln says to Nana.

"What brings you here, Lincoln? Any news?"

There's a pause and we all wait to hear what Lincoln has to say. It takes time for Lincoln to get his words out. I think he's like me, deciding *say it, don't say it, say it, don't say it*. Dad says Lincoln has always chosen his words carefully.

"The town well is drying up, and other wells, too."

We wait again, because we know there's more coming. That's how Lincoln talks. One thought at a time.

"I'm getting calls people are running sludgy water from their faucets."

We're all as quiet as Lincoln then, except for the creaking of the chains on Birdie's swing. We know about the hardships that come with dry wells. Dad and Lincoln get the calls from people whose shallow-dug wells go dry in the summer and they have no water to flush toilets or take baths with, no water to put out fires, no water for cows and horses, chickens and goats and sheep. There are also people who have no wells at all and have to haul water from springs or from their neighbors' houses.

"Some of those calls are hot-tempered" is the last thing Lincoln says before he leaves.

Dad stands by the window and pulls back the curtain. The National Guard is setting up a line of floodlights along the road. Braggy's bulldozer is parked near the edge of the water.

"Harlan," Nana says to Dad, "the way you're looking out the window reminds me of when you were a little boy watching to see how much snow was falling during a blizzard. You'd be the last one to bed, staying up until it was too dark or the snow was swirling too hard to see."

"I guess I did," Dad admits. "I remember some pretty big storms."

"What about me? What did I do when I was little?" I ask Nana.

"When you were a baby, Henry, what you liked best was rocks. Your mom would bring you here for a visit and set you in the shade under your great-grandfather's apple tree. You'd sit right there and put pebbles in your mouth. You never swallowed a one. Then you'd spit them out, all wet and shiny, and pile them up like miniature rain-washed stone walls."

"I don't remember that," I say, but I guess it's true.

"Tell ME." Birdie comes up behind me with her quilt. I didn't realize she was listening to the stories.

"You?" I say. "I remember when you were a baby, Birdie. Your face was very red. And you screamed really loud. Then I held you up to the window so you could see the sky, and you stopped crying. Can you say 'Henry showed me the sky'?"

"I scream," Birdie says, and she seems satisfied with her story. She goes and lies down on the couch in the living room and covers herself with her quilt. Then she gets up again.

"Get Lilygirl," she tells us.

Dad and I look at each other.

"I checked the house but I couldn't find her. Where *is* Lilygirl?" I ask Birdie.

"Sleeping," Birdie says.

"I looked in your bed, Birdie. She wasn't there."

"Mama bed," Birdie explains.

"I didn't look in your bed," I tell Dad. "Can we run back and check?"

"No, it's getting dark. Birdie," Dad says to her. "We'll get Lilygirl tomorrow."

"NO. NOW!" Birdie starts to cry, big tears running down her face, her mouth wide open. Watching her cry for Lilygirl gives me a sick feeling in my stomach. Why didn't I think to look under Mom and Dad's covers?

Mom wraps Birdie's quilt around her and picks her up. She pats her back and sings to her, one song after another, until Birdie's eyes close and her head falls on Mom's shoulder.

"What do you think is going to happen?" I ask Dad.

"Water is a force to be reckoned with—that's what you always say, right?"

"Yes." My father lets the curtain close. "And until this water finds its own level, there is nothing we can do but wait."

"If the meteorite broke through into an aquifer, like you said, how much water is there in an aquifer?"

"I don't know. They're huge storehouses of water. That water could have been underground for thousands and thousands of years."

"If the basement floods, will we have to sell the meteorite to fix the water damage? A museum in New York City once paid forty thousand dollars for a really big meteorite like ours."

"You don't say! That much? I'm not sure what kind of work the house will need, Henry," my father answers.

I feel seventy-five percent glad I told Dad how much money the meteorite could be worth, but also twenty-five percent sorry it might make him feel different about the stone. Then I remember something that happened last summer.

"You know that man from Massachusetts who wanted to buy the old granite foundation stones on Nana's land to decorate his wife's flower garden? Nana said your great-grandfather cut and quarried the granite and built the foundation with his own hands. She said some things aren't for sale. Remember?"

My father reaches his hand out to the curtain again, then pulls it back. If I had to guess, he's eighty percent thinking about the water and our house and twenty percent thinking about everything else. I try to get his attention.

"You wouldn't sell the compass your father gave you on the yard sale table."

Dad takes the brass compass with its leather strap out of his pocket and holds it up in front of him.

"That's true, I wouldn't," he agrees.

"There you are, Henry!" James runs into the kitchen. "Your mom called my dad and he was asked to pick up a night shift, so he said I could stay over and take the bus from here in the morning. I helped her make the beds upstairs. Do you want to stay in the room your father and Braggy used to share? There's two beds in there."

"Okay," I tell James.

"We should all get what sleep we can," Dad says.

"Are you going to drink your water?" I ask him.

"What?"

"The glass of water you drink every night, and the one you take to bed?"

"Sure, Henry."

Dad doesn't move to the sink, so I pour water into the canning jars Nana uses for glasses. I give him one jar, and he drinks it down. I drink mine, too. And I fill both our jars again.

"Good night, Dad," I say.

"Good night, Henry," he answers, but doesn't move away from the window.

Nana sleeps downstairs in a room off the living room, where she doesn't have so many stairs to climb, but the farmhouse has a second floor with two bedrooms. The room my father and Braggy shared has a window that faces down the hill in the direction of the water. It also has a wooden desk and two dressers.

"They're setting up more lights." James has his forehead on the window glass. "Don't you wish we could get a ride in the helicopter and see what it looks like from way up high?"

"Yeah, I'd like to see what the big rock looks like from the sky," I agree, watching out the window with James until it's too dark for us to see anything except the glow of the lights and people-shaped shadows passing back and forth in front of them.

I hope the water doesn't get too high in the basement, since Mom keeps her canning jars on shelves down there, but I'm even more worried that the water will flood the ground around the meteorite and I won't be able to see it or find it anymore.

The M encyclopedia has stories about meteorites that burned the trees around them as they landed, and meteorites that crashed into people's cars, but nothing about a rock that caused a flood.

There are billions of galaxies. Did the stone come from a watery galaxy, full of colors, and is it bringing the water to make itself feel at home, the way I brought my pillow with me to Nana's house? If that's true, how much water will it take for the rock to feel at home here on Bower Hill Road?

CHAPTER ELEVEN

The largest meteorite "in captivity,"
Ahnighito, is so heavy that it is supported by
six pillars that go down to bedrock.
—ASHTON APPLEWHITE, *AMERICAN MUSEUM OF*
NATURAL HISTORY: THE ULTIMATE GUIDE

THE SUN RISES in the east coming up Bower Hill, and as the sky lightens, Mom and Dad and James and Birdie and I walk down to the house. James's father called this morning to say school was canceled because of the flooding. Mom said James could stay with us while Wendell was working at the mill. Nana's knees are aching, so she rests at home. For once, Birdie doesn't ask anyone to carry her. She walks down the hill by herself, dragging her quilt behind her on the ground. No one reminds her to pick it up.

"Go home," Birdie tells us. "Get Lilygirl."

We stop at the concrete barricades the National Guard set up. The house is gone. Where our house once stood is water as far as you can see. In the churning water, boards and shingles and insulation are spinning downstream. A few inches of rust-colored chimney stick out, and more chimney bricks lie along the new muddy banks of the stream. Yellow and green currents shimmer where the sun shines on the fast-moving water. Bower Four and Bower Five, the land for my house when I'm older, are now a cascading stream of color and the wreckage from our house.

"Is the house really gone?" I ask. I know what I'm seeing, but it's still hard to believe. Mom stands very still beside me.

"Yes." She puts a hand on my shoulder, and it feels like she's steadying herself.

"Is the garden gone?" I ask.

"Yes."

"The blackberry patch?"

"Yes."

"My stone wall?" We both look in the same direction.

"Yes," we say at the same time.

"Sing, Mama." Birdie pulls on Mom's coat sleeve.

"Sing what?" Mom asks her.

"'Moon River,'" Birdie says.

"Oh my. All right, Birdie." Mom's true songbird of a voice softly sings one of Birdie's favorite bedtime songs.

When Mom stops singing, she picks up a small, round stone, reaches her arm over the barricade, and lets the pebble fall into the water. The stone immediately sinks out of sight. Mom sits down on the ground and covers her eyes with her hands. Dad walks back and forth, back and forth, next to the water.

"Part of the house is still there," I say to Mom. "It's just underwater."

"Peekaboo, Mama." Birdie laughs and covers her own eyes with her hands. "Peekaboo me."

Mom doesn't answer.

James gathers pebbles in a pile and tries to hit the sticking-out chimney with them. He makes a pile of stones for Birdie. The first one she throws bounces off the barricade, and the second one hits one of the National Guardsmen on his boot. He jumps to the side.

"Good shot, Birdie," James cheers, no matter what she hits.

"Henry." James winds up to throw another pebble. "You get to live on top of the hill now. Even higher than Braggy and Lincoln's houses. And you'll have your own stream to swim in. Maybe we could build a raft. See, Birdie"—James points out in front of us—"you have a stream now."

"Go swim," Birdie says.

"It's too cold to swim now, but if I brought my fishing rod, we could fish for treasure from your house! What do you think, Birdie?"

"Get Lilygirl." Birdie suddenly remembers her duck.

I know I have to think fast before she starts crying again.

"Birdie, maybe Lilygirl is swimming. We can watch the water and see if we see her. Then we can pull her out."

Birdie stares at me, and her mouth opens. I gesture to James to say something.

"That's right," James quickly agrees. "Ducks can

swim! I'm gonna keep my eye on the water, and if I see Lilygirl, I'll lean over and grab her by the beak! What do you think she'd say about that? 'Quackety quack'?"

James squeezes his lips to make the quacking sound, and Birdie laughs in spite of herself.

I'm grateful to James, but my eyes and mind are divided. Fifty percent thinking about Mom sitting so still on the ground and Lilygirl and our house and fifty percent thinking about the big rock.

"What about the meteorite? Can you still see it?" I ask one of the National Guard officers.

She brings her binoculars up to her eyes.

"I believe it's still visible. Here, take a look."

I never looked through binoculars before. They make everything bigger and sharper. The meteorite looks so close in the lens of the binoculars, I feel like I can reach out and touch it. It's unchanged—sitting shiny and black in its crater. If I turned the binoculars around, would the rock see me as clearly as I see it?

"I'm very sorry," the woman says to us. "We tried to bulldoze trenches to divert the water away from the house, but they kept overflowing. We also laid sandbags around the house, but the water just surged over them."

"We thank you for trying, and for all your hard work. This water is not like any I've seen before," Dad says.

I hold the binoculars up to my face again. Something

I didn't see before moves behind the rock. It's just for a second, and the sun hasn't completely risen, but I only know one person with a green-and-black-plaid coat like that.

"That's for sure. We're also getting reports of water levels dropping in local wells. That's unusual for this time of year—"

I interrupt her.

"Can you please let me past? I have to go to the rock. I know the way and I promise I'll be careful."

"Is that safe?" Dad asks the woman.

"Yes, there's a solid path uphill from the water. And I'll keep my eyes on the boy," she says.

I give the heavy binoculars back to the woman and make my way around the barricades.

I wish I still had the binoculars. It's amazing how you can see faraway things right in front of you. It's like having the eyesight of an eagle or a hawk. As I get closer to the rock, I hear a tap-tap-tapping noise. Its rhythm sounds like the big redheaded woodpeckers that peck at tree bark looking for ants. They tap for a while, take a break, then start up again.

Mr. Ronnie, in his green-and-black-plaid coat, is on his knees behind the meteorite. He has a long chisel in one hand and a hammer in the other, and he's striking the top of the chisel with the hammer against the side of the big rock. His eyeglasses are all the way down his nose, and his hat is almost off his head.

"STOP!" I yell. "STOP RIGHT NOW. What are you doing? Leave the stone alone."

Mr. Ronnie is so startled he drops his tools with a loud clank. He pushes his glasses up and pulls his hat down.

"Calm down, son, no harm done. I'm just trying to get a little piece, a little souvenir. Is that a problem?"

"I said you need to STOP."

I lean over to check what Mr. Ronnie did to the meteorite.

"See?" He points to a few silver streaks on the shiny black surface. "I can't even chip off a rat toenail's worth. It's harder than hell. This thing is evil. They should have a reward for getting rid of it."

"EVIL? The rock isn't evil. How can a rock be evil?"

"Look, young man, if you haven't noticed, pieces of your house are floating down to who knows where. What's left of it is underwater and the road is wrecked. What else but this rock caused the flooding and made the town well go dry? If the water doesn't come back downtown, all the stores are gonna go out of business. Including my Picker Palace. Do you call that good?"

"No, I don't think those things are good. But the rock doesn't mean to hurt anyone."

"You bet it's not good." Mr. Ronnie shakes his finger at me. "I hear you Bowers have all the water you need. My son, Dwayne, says it's not a coincidence the rock is here on this hill full of water witchers. Are you one of those water witchers yourself?"

This is the second time in three days I've been asked if I can dowse, and I'm no closer to knowing the answer to the question.

"I don't know," I say. "I've never tried."

"I thought it was in the blood. How you gonna know if you never try?" Mr. Ronnie gathers up his tools. "I suppose you folks still haven't put in for the reward? Must be nice to afford to let it rot there. All I'm saying is you and your family better watch out or you'll be sorry. People are talking."

This time he doesn't wait for me to answer. I would have explained that rocks crumble and break or erode but they don't rot. That Braggy has Bower blood but he can't dowse. Mr. Ronnie turns and makes his way past the water pulsing out of the ground.

I take a big breath and hold it until Mr. Ronnie is out of sight. I think about our house flooding and the town well going dry, Birdie's openmouthed crying for Lilygirl, and Mom covering her eyes. And the pieces of our house floating in the water. It makes me mad that the best thing that ever happened, the meteorite landing, also made the worst thing happen.

Then I get an idea.

I run up to Braggy's shed and find his longest pry bar. The only person who ever tried to move the rock is Birdie with her hands, and she's two years old. I've got a hard metal lever that's taller than I am, and the ground is soft now.

At the edge of the field I find a rock big enough for a fulcrum to rest the lever on. I've seen Dad move big rocks this way, using one rock and a lever to move another rock.

If I can tip the rock forward and set it rolling down the hill, the meteorite might land downhill from Bower Four. It could have Bower Five. Or Bower Six. It could draw up the water from there instead. Then maybe the water over our house would dry up.

If the stone-wall basement is still standing, Dad could build a new house on it, in the same place as the old one.

If the water dried up now, maybe we'd find some of the things that hadn't gotten washed away yet.

If the bottom surface of the rock is flat and just resting on the ground, and the soil is soft, maybe I can wedge the lever right underneath it.

That's a lot of ifs.

On the uphill side of the meteorite, at the bottom edge of the rock, I push the heavy pry bar into the ground until it won't go in any more. I position the fulcrum rock under the bar.

I lean on the top end of the pry bar as hard as I can, hanging my whole weight on it, half on either side. From where I hang, I see the meteorite upside down—the beautiful black shiny crust and the glints of metal. It seems like the rock is waiting to see what I'll do next. I feel how patient it is.

Will I push it down the hill?

Will I pull the pry bar out and bang it on the meteorite like Mr. Ronnie did with his chisel and hammer?

It might have waited more than a million human lifetimes before it slowed down enough to land.

It was struck before, by whatever made the thumbprint-shaped marks on its surface.

Still hanging there, I think about the night I watched it arc across the field, and how it lay there in the snow the next morning. My anger leaves me, and as it does, I feel the bar loosen. I get off and pull it out of the ground. I don't know what I was thinking. It would probably take a lever as tall as a pine tree to move the rock.

I need a better plan.

"Sorry," I say, touching the side of the meteorite, "I know you're not evil. I know you didn't mean to flood our house."

I notice an empty Styrofoam cup Mr. Ronnie must have dropped lying near the rock, and I fill it with water right where it comes out of the ground. Holding the cup of water in one hand and the pry bar in the other, I make my way back up the hill to Braggy's shed and then toward Nana's.

James and Birdie are still throwing pebbles into the water where our house was. I hear James's excited cheers from across the field. I don't think James gets it from Wendell, his dad, but I wonder if James's mother was also a one hundred percent kind of person.

Nana is napping in the recliner in the living room, snoring with each in-and-out breath.

I pour the water from the Styrofoam cup into a canning jar and set it on the counter. I want to see what happens if I shine a bright light into the jar of water. Will I be able to see any other colors besides yellow and green? I go looking for a flashlight in the garage, which is attached to the house by a covered walkway.

While I'm searching, the house phone rings once, twice, three times. I wait to see if Nana gets it, but it keeps ringing four, five, six times, so I run back into the house. Nana is slowly pushing herself up out of the recliner.

"Would you get that, dear? My hip bone is sore this morning."

I run to the phone that hangs from the wall next to the front door.

"Hello?"

"I would like to speak with a Mr. Henry Bower. Is this his home?" It's a man's voice that speaks with an accent I've never heard before.

"Yes, that's me. I'm Henry Bower. But this is my nana's home you called."

"Ah, quite a few Bowers listed for your town. No one answered at the other residences."

"My uncles Lincoln and Braggy are outside with the National Guard, and my house is underwater."

"Well, that illuminates the situation. May I introduce myself? I am Dr. Miles Morgan, curator of the meteorite collection at the American Museum of Natural History in New York City. Central Park West at Seventy-Ninth Street, to be exact."

"Where the Ahnighito meteorite is? The one the Inuit called the Tent?"

"That is correct. You have visited the museum?"

"No, but I saw pictures in the M encyclopedia, and I read about how the Ahnighito is almost as old as the sun, and that it fell in Greenland. Parts of it look like our rock."

"Your M encyclopedia is quite informative. And that brings me to the purpose of this call. I was made aware of your find by a colleague of mine, who read about it this morning in an article the *New York Times* reprinted from your local paper."

"It's in our paper?"

"Oh yes, the headline says, and I quote, 'Homeschooled Maine Rock Boy Finds Possible Meteorite in Back Field.' Fortunately, they provided the name of that Maine rock boy, one Henry Bower. Did you not see this story?"

"No, my uncle Braggy gets the paper and shares it with us when he's done," I explain. "Were you there when Admiral Peary brought the Ahnighito to the museum?"

"I am considered elderly by some, but that occurred long before I was born. However, I have been closely acquainted with it for more than half my mortal life."

It isn't just the accent. The words the man uses are

different from what I'm used to hearing. They remind me of some of the long words I've seen in the old red books Birdie takes out of the library.

"Can I ask you a question? And I don't mean to sound rude."

"Certainly. I am not one to be easily offended," the man answers in his odd way.

"Does everyone in New York City talk like you?"

Dr. Miles Morgan laughs so long and hard that I'm not sure if I said something funny or if I've insulted him. Finally, he stops laughing.

"I was born and raised in the United Kingdom, in the town of Nottingham. So no, I am most certainly not a representative of the natural dialect of New York City, if there is one. But I did not call to waste your time, Henry Bower. I rang to communicate that the entire team of the meteoritic collection here at the natural history museum, myself included, naturally, appreciates your apparent consideration for this unique find and will employ all that we have to offer in the way of science and information."

"You read about the reward?" I ask Miles Morgan.

"Yes, I did. I read that a substantial sum is being offered by a private collector."

"But you want to take the meteorite for *your* museum?"

"Not at all. I'm a scientist, not a thief."

"Would you like to come see it?" I ask, surprising myself.

There's a pause on the other end of the phone, and while I wait for Dr. Miles Morgan to answer, I turn toward the kitchen just in time to see Nana swallow the last of the water from the canning jar I set by the sink.

CHAPTER TWELVE

Earth is nicknamed the Blue Planet because
seventy percent of it is covered in water.
—KIMBERLY M. HUTMACHER,
STUDYING OUR EARTH, INSIDE AND OUT

I DROP THE PHONE and it spins around on the waxed linoleum kitchen floor.

"Nana! That was my rock water. The water coming out of the ground."

"Oh, gracious, I thought it tasted different. Sweet and salty at the same time. Reminds me of when my father collected sap and we boiled our tea with it. I'm afraid I didn't leave any for you, Henry. Drank it right down."

"That's okay, Nana, I can get more, but I don't know if it's good for you to drink."

"Dad said there was no water better than spring water, coming right out of the earth. Never hurt a fly."

I grab the phone off the floor.

"Sorry, Dr. Morgan. I dropped the phone."

"I concluded that, based on the clatter in my ear. Thank you, Henry. I *would* like to accept your kind invitation. I can arrive tomorrow around twelve noon if that is convenient."

"That would be great. Do you know where we live?" I ask Dr. Morgan.

"It says in the paper that you live on Bower Hill Road in Lowington, Maine."

"That's right. We're the first house at the top of the hill after you pass the cemetery and the granite quarry and the gravel pit."

"And will there be signs for these attractions?"

"Signs? No, but you can't get lost because the water is flooding the road past us."

"That's a comfort, I suppose. I look forward to meeting you and your family. I will ring off now and make my travel arrangements. Thank you, Henry Bower," Dr. Miles Morgan says, and hangs up the phone before I can answer.

"We have company coming tomorrow, Nana. The curator from the American Museum of Natural History in New York City, where the Ahnighito is. It's the heaviest meteorite ever moved by humans, and they had to build a stand for it that went down to the bedrock under the museum. He says he'll be here around noon. He wants to see the stone."

"Oh my. A visitor all the way from New York City. Do you think he'd like baked beans and biscuits for a noon-hour meal?"

"Sure, he's coming a long way. Thanks, Nana."

In some ways, Nana is like the big stone. No matter what's happening around her, she stays the same. She takes ketchup and two onions out of the refrigerator. I realize she was asleep in her recliner this morning and doesn't know what happened to our house.

"Nana, I have bad news. The water washed away our house."

"Henry, don't joke about something like that." Nana frowns at me.

"I'm not, Nana. Nothing's there anymore. No house, no garden, no stone wall. It's all covered in water."

"Oh no. All gone?" Nana sounds like Birdie. She stands there still holding the onions and ketchup.

"Yes, the only thing you can see is the top of the chimney," I answer, "and pieces of the house all in the water."

"Who would have thought the water would do that?" Even though you can't see the stream from the kitchen window that faces the road, Nana goes over and stands there looking out. I wait for her to say something else, but she's completely quiet.

I close my eyes and try to imagine I'm still in my own house, but I can't do it. Our house smelled like the pinecones Mom used to start fires, and the herbs she hung from the kitchen ceiling. Nana's house smells like old wallpaper and the cream she rubs on her knees. I sniffed near the walls when I was little and figured out that was where the house smell was coming from. Dad says it's something called menthol in the knee cream that makes my eyes burn and stays in the air.

Nana's house is like the replica. It's what we're left with now instead of our real house.

"Are you okay, Henry?" Nana asks.

Before I can answer, the door slams and I open my eyes. Mom and Dad and Birdie come in.

"Where's James?" I ask.

"Wendell picked him up. But he'll be staying over tomorrow night," Mom says. Instead of helping Nana in the kitchen or putting wood in the stove, she goes into the living room and sits down on the couch. I'm not used to seeing Mom just sitting in the middle of the day unless she's sick.

"Are you getting sick?" I ask her.

Mom puts a hand on her cheek, like she's checking her temperature.

"I don't think so. Why?" she asks.

"Just wondering," I answer.

I remember the phone call from Dr. Morgan.

"A scientist from the museum in New York City is coming tomorrow. Around twelve noon. To see the stone," I announce.

Birdie gives me a pebble from her pocket.

"Throw stone," she tells me.

Out of habit, I bring the pebble to my nose, but all I can smell are the onions Nana is cutting up.

"Isn't that something," Dad says. He goes in and out of the house, bringing kindling and firewood from the woodshed, armload after armload. Then he fills the pans of water on the stove. After that, he looks around like he's not sure what to do next.

"He grew up in Nottingham, England," I add.

I want to ask Dad what the plan is now. All the floating pieces of our house can't be put together to rebuild our home. The rock-wall basement Dad laid stone by stone is probably part of the streambed now. I have socks but no shirts except the one I'm wearing. Dad and Braggy's old bedroom opens into a long hallway, not a kitchen like at home. And since the bedroom is upstairs, I won't be able to hear the sounds of the wood stove being filled before I go to sleep, or the crackling of the firewood burning during the night.

We're all out of order. Our family on Bower One instead of Four, higher up the hill than Lincoln and Braggy, and no dry land past Bower Four for me and Birdie to build our houses on when we're older.

"Henry, would you stir these beans for me?" Nana asks.

I stand at the cookstove and stir the simmering beans with Nana's long-handled spoon while she adds the salt, pepper, ketchup, and salt pork, but I turn so Nana can't see my face. For once, I'm not happy to be here.

Mom hasn't moved from the couch.

"I wish I'd taken your mother's rings and dishes and Birdie's crib mattress," I hear Dad say to Mom. "I really thought we'd be back to mop up the water and dry out the house."

I can't hear what Mom says.

I wish I'd taken the rest of my clothes and my books and my rock collection.

I especially wish I'd found Lilygirl.

Nana leans over and starts to whisper in my ear, "You know, Henry, you all can—" but I stop her.

"Please don't say it, Nana," I tell her. "I know what you're going to say, but please don't say it."

Nana opens her mouth, then closes it. Maybe she understands that I don't want to hear how we can always stay at Bower One. Sometime, I know, she will say it, but I just don't want it to be today.

"Not today, anyway," I add, so her feelings won't be hurt.

"Okay, Henry." Nana is quiet for a minute, watching me stir the beans. "How about you bring your mother a sandwich."

She takes a spoonful of egg salad from a bowl in the refrigerator, smooths it out on a piece of white bread, adds a slice of tomato, and covers it with another slice of bread. She puts it on a plate and I take it over to Mom. Birdie leans against Mom on the couch.

Mom takes the top piece of bread and the tomato off the sandwich and stares at it like she's never seen an egg salad sandwich before. She picks up the other half, takes a few bites, and hands the plate back to me.

Sometimes when a big snowstorm was coming, we stayed at Nana's house, but we always had our house to go home to the next day. Tonight feels different. Mom and Dad sleep in the other upstairs bedroom, Uncle Lincoln's old room. Birdie sleeps there, too, on a couch cushion Dad brought up for her.

I wake up during the night and I'm confused, thinking my bed got turned around and the windows are in the wrong place. Then I realize I'm at Nana's house.

Thump thump thump Thump thump thump.

A thumping sound comes from downstairs.

Thump thump thump Thump thump thump.

I tiptoe to the top of the stairs and look down into the living room. Dad is pacing back and forth like he did down by the water. I tiptoe quietly back down the hall.

Dad is like a nocturnal animal, awake when everyone else is asleep. Mom is like an animal going into hibernation, eating less and slowing down her movements to conserve energy.

In my father's old room, I push the bed so it's up against the wall in the same direction my bed was at home. It's colder in here than in my bedroom at home, so I take the blankets off the second bed and pile them over myself. I get my notebook from my backpack. There's a pencil marking the page where I wrote my last question.

Is the other mammoth tusk still in the mud?

I imagine digging in the old drainage pond in Scarborough and suddenly hitting something as hard as the antler James found on the snow as I uncover the second real tusk. It would be like the moment I stood on the roof and watched the meteorite flash across the sky.

I pick up the pencil and write:

When it traveled through the universe, did the meteorite ever pass anything that was alive?

The extra blankets finally warm me enough to go back to sleep. I put my notebook and pencil down and turn out the light. Twelve noon can't come fast enough.

CHAPTER THIRTEEN

Meteorites have enabled us to come close to
answering questions such as "How did the Earth,
Sun and planets form?", and even
"How did we come to be here?"
—ROBERT HUTCHINSON AND ANDREW GRAHAM,
METEORITES

I WISH I'D ASKED Miles Morgan the color of
his car so I could be sure not to miss him coming over the
hill. I put on my coat and hat and go out on the porch to
wait.

The Lowington Fire Department water tanker truck is
down where the moving water crosses the road, filling up.
Dad and Lincoln and Braggy help fill plastic barrels in the
back of a pickup truck with a hose connected to a gen-
erator. Birdie stands there in her red coat watching them.
Mom is upstairs in Lincoln's old bedroom, resting again.

I guess that Dr. Miles Morgan's car will be silver, then
I guess black, then red, and then a very ordinary dark
blue car pulls into the driveway.

The driver's-side door opens and Dr. Miles Morgan
steps out. His skin is a lighter shade of the meteorite, and

he wears a gray suit, a white shirt, and a red tie. His shoes are black and shiny. I've only seen men wear clothes like these at my grandfather's funeral. He doesn't wear a coat or a hat, and he carries a briefcase.

The wind at the top of the hill blows strong and cold, good for keeping the frost from hitting the garden, but not good for city men wearing thin clothes in February. Dr. Miles Morgan shivers as he looks up at Nana's big farmhouse, painted white but peeling from years of wind and snow.

"Hello, Dr. Morgan. Welcome." I hold out my hand.

Dr. Morgan's hand is cold. He looks around at the patches of snow still in Nana's fields and the leafless maples in front of the house. Smoke rises straight up from the chimney, and you can taste it in the air.

"What a spectacularly wintry landscape you have here," he says.

"It *is* winter," I explain.

He takes a cell phone out of his pocket and holds it up.

"There doesn't appear to be any cell phone service here," he says.

"There's no cell phone service in most of Lowington," I say, and lead the way into Nana's warm kitchen.

Dr. Miles Morgan is nothing like Mr. Ronnie. He sits at Nana's kitchen table for an hour and doesn't ask a single question about the meteorite. He doesn't ask how big it is.

He doesn't ask where it is. He doesn't ask to go see it. He's most interested in Nana's baked beans and biscuits. After eating two biscuits, then two more, covering them with so much butter you can hardly see the biscuits, Dr. Morgan takes a small leather notebook and a fountain pen out of his briefcase.

"Would you be so kind as to share your recipe for these delightfully flaky scones?" He holds a biscuit up between two fingers.

"These biscuits? I just take some flour . . . ," Nana starts to explain.

"And how much might that be?"

"Why, enough to leave room in the bowl for shortening and milk."

"Ah, and the shortening?"

"Crisco. Don't you have that in New York City?"

"Yes, we most certainly do. And how might you measure that?"

"I add enough of the Crisco and milk so it doesn't stick to the bowl. And some salt. Just a few shakes. With the baking powder."

Dr. Morgan stops writing and closes his notebook. He takes another biscuit.

"I see. You are a natural cook. That is a rare thing," he tells Nana.

"Is that your science notebook?" I point to the leather book. "I have a homeschool notebook."

"No, this is my daily planner. It helps me keep track of those many tedious appointments and meetings," the curator says.

I take my notebook out of my backpack, open it to the pages about the meteorite, and lay it on the table next to Dr. Morgan's plate. No one has ever read my notebooks. It's like the Honor Box. Mom trusts what I write in it.

"You can read my notebook if you want," I tell him. "This is the only one I have left. Numbers six, seven, eight, and nine were on my bookshelf at home when the water washed everything away."

Dr. Morgan takes one more bite of his biscuit, puts it down on his plate, and starts reading my notebook. At some of the pages, he nods his head, at others he puts his finger under a line of my writing like he's really thinking about what's written there.

While he's reading, Nana pours him another cup of coffee. He scoops three teaspoons of sugar into his cup and sips it as he reads.

"Hmmm." He hums to himself, reading, and when he's done, he closes the notebook and lays his hand on the cover.

"Henry, I see you've been asking yourself many of the same questions I have over the years. What is most important is not always the answers, but the questions. Keep asking the questions. Which isn't as simple as it seems, to devise the kind of questions and observations that will lead to answers."

I'm thinking the answers have to be important, too. Like, why dowsing works for some people and not others, and if there's a secret dowsing sense that a scientist could find if he knew where to look. Or why a rock brings enough water to flood a road. But I don't want the curator to think I'm being rude.

Before I have a chance to say anything, Dad and Birdie come into the house.

"This is Dr. Miles Morgan," I say. "He's in charge of the meteorites at the American Museum of Natural History in New York City. And he came all the way here because he saw an article in the paper about the rock."

"Welcome." Dad shakes his hand. "Harlan Bower."

"I'm Boss," Birdie tells the curator.

"This is my sister, Birdie," I explain. " 'The Boss' is her nickname."

"I'm three," Birdie adds.

"On your birthday this summer, then you'll be three," I remind her.

"Three now," Birdie repeats.

"Okay, Birdie." Ever since we came to Bower One, Birdie acts older, walking instead of wanting to be carried, swinging by herself on Nana's swing instead of asking to be pushed, even shouting less. I know our house is really gone, but I'm not sure Birdie does.

"Mom," I call up the stairs, "the curator from the museum is here."

Mom comes down the stairs slowly.

"Alice Bower, pleased to meet you," she says to the curator.

Dr. Morgan opens his briefcase on the table.

"I appreciate the hospitality you've shown me on such short notice, and I want to present you all with some gifts from the museum."

For the second time in three days, there is gift-giving at Nana's house.

"Shall we choose youngest first?" Miles Morgan asks, and gives Birdie three postcards.

"I am not sure of your personal preferences, but these are some of our most popular cards."

"No, THAT." Birdie hands the postcards back to Dr. Morgan and points to his neck.

"Oh, Birdie." I turn to Dr. Morgan. "She wants your tie. Because it's red. That's her favorite color. Birdie, that's part of Dr. Morgan's clothes."

"My tie?" Miles Morgan touches a hand to his tie.

"Red tie." Birdie nods.

Miles Morgan unknots his tie and holds it out to Birdie. She lifts her chin and points to her neck.

"She wants you to put it on her, the way you wore it," I tell the curator.

"Dr. Morgan, you don't have to give Birdie your tie," Mom says.

"Put on," Birdie says, softly this time, and Miles Morgan kneels down and places the tie around her neck. He crosses one end over the other, loops it up and over, knots it carefully, and adjusts it so it isn't too loose or too tight.

Birdie throws herself at Dr. Morgan and hugs him.

Next out of Dr. Morgan's briefcase is a five-hundred-piece dinosaur puzzle for Nana, free passes to the museum for all of us, and T-shirts that say AMERICAN MUSEUM OF NATURAL HISTORY on them.

"Thank you, Dr. Morgan." Nana studies the stegosaurus on the cover of the puzzle box. "I love puzzles, but I never had a dinosaur one."

"Henry, I brought something special for you." The curator unzips a small compartment inside the briefcase and passes me a plastic bag.

"This is from my personal collection."

I lift the bag so the sun coming through the low farmhouse windows shines on the little pebble inside.

I study it through the plastic bag.

"It looks like our rock," I say.

Dr. Morgan clears his throat and looks into his empty coffee cup. Despite his missing tie, and his shirt having come loose from his pants when he kneeled down to put the tie on Birdie, he still looks very dignified.

"Dr. Morgan, would you like some more coffee?" Nana asks him.

"Certainly, thank you kindly. This was an unusually early morning for me."

"I'll get it, Mom," Dad says. "Save your knees the trip."

"Why, my knees feel good as new right now! Not a bit of an ache."

I take the stone out of the bag. It fits in the palm of my hand and looks like a miniature version of the rock in the field. It's surprisingly heavy for its size, with a single thumbprint-shaped ridge on one side and a few specks of shiny metal. Its fusion crust is black and shiny but flaked away in places, and the underneath rock is gray and pitted.

"It's heavy for a stone this small," I say.

"I suspect it contains a high percentage of metal. The Hoba meteorite, for instance, the heaviest one we know, is made up of eighty-four percent iron and sixteen percent nickel."

Dad leans over the table to get a better look at the stone. I hold it out for Mom to see, too. She strokes it with one finger. I bring the stone up to my nose, but it doesn't smell like the stone in our field. Maybe the stone lost its smell over the years.

"What else is the stone from your collection made of? And where did you get it?" I ask the curator.

"There you are, Henry. Very good questions. To answer your first question, I believe it contains elements so rare they have not been identified yet. I call it the water rock."

"What does that mean? None of the rock books in our library have anything about a water rock."

The curator sits back in his chair and clasps his hands.

"Perhaps one day there will be such a book. Perhaps you, Henry Bower, will write that book. To answer your second question, as to how this stone came into my possession, I must share a tale of young Miles Morgan. Would you all be interested to hear it?" the curator asks us.

"Yes, we would," I say, and Mom and Dad and Nana wait quietly for the curator to speak. Birdie swings on her swing, the red tie going up and down.

"Growing up in Nottingham, I was a sickly child; the doctor said I did not have a strong constitution. I was thin, not like I am now"—Dr. Morgan pats his round stomach and the tight belt over it—"and I coughed in the night. Consequently, I was kept out of school quite often, and left on my own during the day, whilst my parents worked. I occupied myself by reading and looking out the window onto our crowded street. One fateful morning I heard a loud rumble of noise overhead, and a small stone broke through our parlor window and landed on the floor in front of me."

I feel the stone's shape in my hand.

"A meteorite from a fireball?" I guess.

"You are absolutely correct. One and the same. I attribute the entire trajectory of my life to that moment."

Dr. Morgan pauses and looks around the room. He enjoys telling his story a lot more than I liked telling my secret into the microphone.

"What happened after it came through your window?" I ask.

"For one, I could not convince my parents that it was not I who had broken that pane. Even showing them the culprit"—Dr. Morgan points to the stone in the bag—"did not persuade them. I was, after all, only a ten-year-old boy at the time, with no advanced degrees in geology."

The curator gets up from his chair, as if his story is too big to be told sitting in one place.

"Then things happened, things that have still not been explained. Nottingham's water supply doubled overnight. There was so much water pressure that it filled bathtubs and ran out of faucets on its own. It gushed out of fire hydrants onto the streets. The river Trent overflowed into parks and playgrounds. You can imagine how the children of Nottingham liked that! What eclipsed that event, for my parents, was that I got well. My cough vanished, I put on weight, and I was able to run and play without catching my breath."

The curator holds his arms out to the sides, then pats his cheeks to show us how healthy he is now.

"No other pieces of my water rock were found. My guess is that a large fall, the mother of my fragment, embedded itself somewhere deep in Nottingham's grassy heathland."

"There in Nottingham, England, where you grew up, the stone came, and then the water. But then the flooding stopped, right? How long did it take? And what made it stop?" I ask.

My parents hold their breath, too, waiting for the curator's answer.

"Yes, the flooding did cease. The precise timetable is unclear to me. However, new tributaries formed that flowed into the river Trent and that remain to this day. The water carved its own path through the moorlands and through city streets as well, which are still underwater, like the mythical Atlantis."

"Why can't you figure out what it's made of?"

Dr. Morgan takes a newspaper clipping out of his briefcase and holds it up for us to see. There's a photograph of me standing next to the big rock with my hand stretched out.

"When this article was brought to my attention, I had to use my magnifying glass to see what many may not have noticed. Is that not a magnet in your hand, Henry?"

Which is not exactly an answer to my question. It's a question to my question.

"Yes, I wanted to show how the magnet was attracted to the rock. To prove that it was a meteorite."

"That's when I knew I would be paying a call on a fellow scientist."

I shake my head. "I'm not a scientist. I'm only ten years old."

"I beg to differ. Now, I was hoping it might be an opportune time for me to pay my respects to this stone of yours, Henry. One visitor greeting another, one might say."

CHAPTER FOURTEEN

Fusion crusts on freshly fallen meteorites vary enormously. Often smooth, crusts can also be decorated with spattered droplets, or strings and rivulets of molten material. Rounded pits and depressions resembling thumb prints in a ball of clay are found on the surfaces of many meteorites.

—ALEX BEVAN AND JOHN DE LAETER,
METEORITES: A JOURNEY THROUGH SPACE AND TIME

DAD SQUINTS out the window at the thermometer nailed to a porch post.

"Please take my coat, hat, and winter boots for the walk," Dad says to Miles Morgan. "It's twenty-eight degrees out there and the wind is blowing."

The curator opens his briefcase again, takes out a thin silver camera, and puts it in his inside jacket pocket.

"No thank you, Mr. Bower, though I do appreciate your kind offer of winter apparel. However, I wish to go as I am"—and again the curator holds his arms out to his sides—"when I pay my respects to the stone in question. Will the young lady who fancies red be accompanying us?" the curator asks Birdie.

"Want to go to the big rock?" I translate for Birdie.

Birdie flies out of her swing in an instant, landing on the floor with both feet. She pulls on her own hat and steps into her red boots. Mom helps Birdie into her coat and lets her leave the top button open so she can feel the tie Dr. Morgan gave her.

"All gone," Birdie tells Dr. Morgan. "Swam away."

Mom and Dad and I look at each other.

"All gone," Birdie sings this time. "All gone."

"Are you coming with us, too?" I ask my parents.

"I think I'll lie down for a bit." Mom yawns, even though she didn't wake up that long ago.

"I'm bringing food down to the National Guard and checking on the town well," Dad says.

I lead the way to the meteorite again, but this time it's just me and Miles Morgan and Birdie. She runs ahead, filling her pockets with pebbles.

"That's my uncle Lincoln's house." I point to Bower Two as we pass the small cedar-shingled building. "He's the oldest brother. And the three-story house below it is Uncle Braggy's."

"That *is* a rather tall house for this locale. Though I myself reside on the seventeenth floor."

"SEVENTEENTH FLOOR!" I'm so surprised I stop in my tracks, trying to imagine how high into the sky seventeen floors would take me.

"That is quite commonplace in Manhattan. Building up is a practical solution for limited space. I do have a small balcony with a very fine view of Central Park, but it doesn't compare with the natural beauty you have here."

"Don't tell Braggy about the seventeenth floor. He thinks he lives in the highest house."

"My lips are sealed." The curator holds one finger up to his mouth.

We get to the place where our house was. I can't see the top of the chimney anymore. The only sign that our house was ever there are the bricks and roof shingles washed up next to the water. There isn't any more wood or pieces of the house in the water. They must have washed away. If I could see to the bottom of the stream, would there be all the things that sank down, too heavy to float? Spoons, forks, knives, Dad's cast-iron skillet, the rest of my encyclopedias, the metal ash bucket, our big oak kitchen table?

I'm not holding my breath, but it feels like I am. All the air is trapped in my chest and can't get out. I cough to see if it will help, and it does, a little. Dr. Morgan doesn't seem to notice. He hasn't looked away from the water since we stopped here.

I make a list in my head of the animals I've seen lose their homes.

1. Ants, when I've dug into their holes by accident
2. A robin's nest blown down during a thunderstorm
3. A spider who built its web in the woodshed doorway

Spiders go right to work making new webs, but Mom told me robins sometimes move into an empty nest. I don't know about us. Can we be happy like a robin in a new nest, or are we like the ants I disturbed, going in circles trying to find a way back into their broken tunnels?

I point to the middle of the glittery stream.

"That's where our house used to be. Right there. My father was going to build a porch on in the spring. So Mom could cook down the sap even when it rained."

"All gone," Birdie sings out again, throwing one pebble after another into the water. "Swam away. All gone. Swam away."

"That's right, Birdie, our house is gone," I say. I think she might also be talking about Lilygirl, but I don't want to remind her of her lost duck.

"All gone." She doesn't sing the words this time but says them very seriously.

Dr. Morgan stares at the water that covers our house, and the swirls of green and yellow currents.

"I'm sorry, Henry, that you lost your childhood home. I left mine by choice and I still miss it. But this"—the curator gets right up to the edge of the water—"this is a sight I haven't seen in fifty years. In Nottingham, they dubbed it rainbow water. There were those who claimed it was a fabrication and those who saw the colors clearly. In the midst of the arguments, the colors vanished, never to be seen again. I speculate that the minerals that made the colors were diluted over time."

"What colors were there?"

"Yellows and greens, as well as flashes of red."

"My friend James says it's good we have a stream now. He wants us to build a raft."

"Your mate James is certainly an optimist."

I never heard the word "optimist" used about anyone before. I like that there's a word to explain James's one hundred percent.

"My bedroom faced out toward the big field. When I heard the strange noise, I went up on the roof. That's where I was when the rock landed. Dr. Morgan, what did the other scientists say when you told them about the water rock?"

"That's a tale I have not told before, but I will tell *you*. Once, many years ago, I received a prestigious award for my study of meteorites from Mars. I stood at the podium where I was presented the award and began the acceptance speech I had prepared. I held up that stone you now have in your pocket and recounted the childhood tale I told you and your family. Then I went on to say that I believed that, just as a magnet attracts another magnet, there might be meteorites with a composition that attracts water, perhaps from a planet in a distant galaxy. And when that meteorite gets within Earth's orbit, it is attracted to large bodies of underground fresh water."

"Like what we have here under Bower Hill. And what did they say when you told them that?" I ask the curator, leading him in the direction of the big rock. Birdie runs ahead of us.

"They laughed, Henry. Oh, did they laugh. They thought I was being humorous. In fact, they laughed so long and hard I never did finish my speech. Afterwards, when I left the podium with my award, they slapped me on the back and pronounced me Water Man and told me not to forget to put the stone back in the road where I got it on the way in."

"They didn't understand."

"No, they did not. And because I felt humiliated and disappointed at the reception of my speech, I never again spoke about my water rock theory."

"But you're a scientist. Why didn't you test the meteorite and prove it to them?"

Dr. Morgan doesn't answer, because just then the big rock comes into view, and he stands very still gazing at it.

"What a magnificent specimen, your stone from the sky."

Water bubbles out of the ground around us. Birdie runs to the rock, her red coat billowing out in the wind. Dr. Miles Morgan kneels down, cups both hands together, fills them with water, and tips his hands into his open mouth.

Then he stands, takes the camera out of his pocket, and snaps photographs as he observes the big rock. He steps back to take a picture of the whole rock in its crater and then moves in to take close-ups of the surface of the stone. He talks to himself.

"Fusion crust."

"Regmaglypts."

"Impact crater."

"Metallic flakes."

"Is it as big as the Ahnighito at the museum?" I ask Dr. Morgan.

"It is substantially bigger."

When the curator says our rock is bigger, I understand for the first time the way Braggy must feel when he finds out something he has is larger or taller than someone else's.

As I get closer to the big rock, the little stone in my pocket moves. I make a fist around it and take it out. When I uncurl my fingers, for the second time in a week something jumps from my hand to the rock. The movement of the small pebble is faster and stronger than the magnet. Almost as soon as my hand opens, it's gone.

Dr. Morgan touches the little stone where it landed on the side of the rock.

"Get up." Birdie tries to climb onto the big rock. I give her a lift onto the flat part at the top.

"To answer your question, Henry—if I had tried to analyze the composition of my stone, I would have had to grind it up to test in our machines, and break it apart to send pieces to other scientists to corroborate my results. In effect, destroy the stone that came through my window and somehow restored me to health. That is what scientists do, which perhaps makes me not such an exemplary scientist."

"You *are* exemplary." I'm not exactly sure what the word means, but I know it describes Miles Morgan. "You didn't want a replica of your stone. You wanted to keep the real one. And you would never do *this*. See the scratches Mr. Ronnie made with his chisel?" I show the curator the marks close to the bottom of the meteorite.

"Not to worry, Henry. I highly doubt they are scratches. See . . ." Dr. Morgan dips his crisp white pocket handkerchief into the water around the rock and wipes off the silver streaks. There are no scratches.

"Those were merely pieces of Mr. Ronnie's chisel that the rock wore off," the curator explains.

"Wow! How did you know the marks would come off?"

"That, Henry, is a question I am *not* proud to answer. When I was a lad, I borrowed my mother's favorite ring, without her permission, I must admit. I scraped the little diamond in it across my stone. The only mark that was made was etched right through her diamond, and diamond, as you may know, is a ten on the Mohs hardness scale, much harder than Mr. Ronnie's chisel."

"So no one could chisel off a piece of the stone to get the reward, even if they tried?"

"That is correct. Not with any ordinary implements. However, since that first experiment with my mother's ring, there is one other I've been sorely tempted to perform."

"What's that?" I ask.

"My team has access to a piece of equipment called a mass spectrometer. We take a sample of a meteorite and vaporize it in the device. It is a complicated process, but it enables us to date the meteorites."

"You can figure out how old they are?"

"Yes, and I've always suspected that the water rock may be older than our solar system. But again, due to the small size of the stone, I might be able to date it at the cost of its annihilation."

"BIG BIRDS." Birdie points at the flooded field. I look where she's facing but don't see any birds.

"BRAGGY." Birdie points in the other direction.

"Birdie, what are you doing up there? ROCKin' and rollin'?" Braggy booms.

"No, Braggy," Birdie says from her perch on top of the rock. "BIG BIRDS."

"I came down to say hello to the man from New York City they were all talking about up on the hill. You've come a long way. How far is New York City from here?" Braggy asks Dr. Morgan.

"Approximately six hundred and ten miles," the curator answers.

Miles Morgan's thin dress pants are wet from kneeling by the water, and his shiny leather shoes are muddy. A gold button on his jacket dangles by a thread.

"I've been to Florida," Braggy continues. "Everglades City. One thousand nine hundred fifty miles.

Approximately. My son lives down there. He never liked the cold. I don't mind the cold—or the heat. He wants me to come in the winter but I go in the summer. That's when you get TRIPLE-digit temperatures. Have you ever been to Florida?"

"Yes, I once observed a shuttle launch at Cape Canaveral. But that is not as far south as the Everglades. Very pleased to meet you. Your nephew remarked on your lofty residence."

"It's the only three-story house in Lowington. And I'm thinking of adding a widow's walk on the roof, now that I have a water view." Braggy studies Miles Morgan. "You're sure dressed like you're from Florida, and you've come a long way to see a rock. What do you think? Is Henry's boulder the real thing?"

I watch Dr. Morgan, wondering if he'll answer Braggy's questions, ask him a question of his own, or tell a story. Birdie watches, too, from her lookout on top of the rock, the red tie hanging down over her coat.

"Every day at the museum, packages arrive in the post, with rocks people think might be meteorites. My team has to determine which are meteorites and which are meteorwrongs. That's our little joke! Ninety-nine-point-nine percent of the time, they are nothing more than an unusual river cobble, or a piece of hematite stone, which also attracts a magnet. One time someone even showed up at the museum with a rusted cannonball."

Miles Morgan clasps his hands together in front of him like he did at the house.

"Yes, Mr. Braggy, this stone is without a doubt the real thing, the rare find I dared not hope to see in my lifetime. It is one of the more sizable meteorites to fall in North America. What becomes of this large stone is another story entirely, not mine to tell."

Dr. Miles Morgan turns to me.

"This is your story, Henry Bower, yours and the young lady in red who possesses no fear of heights."

Birdie is not only standing on top of the rock now, she is jumping on one foot and then the other, humming the "Moon River" tune.

"She gets that from me," Braggy tells Dr. Morgan, beating his chest. "No fear here, either."

Miles Morgan blows warm air onto his fingers. He pulls up his sleeve and looks at his watch. "It's later than I thought. I must depart shortly. My flight leaves this evening."

I pry the little stone off the big rock. It doesn't come off as easily as it flew on. I help Birdie down off the meteorite and she skips along next to us. The curator is silent as we head to the house.

Dr. Morgan keeps looking back at the meteorite, as if he wants to fix it in his mind the way I did. Once, he stops, gets out his silver camera, and takes a photograph of the rock in the distance, with the water coursing down below it. I'm quiet, too, and I imagine how the rock called to the underground water. I wonder if it rose to the ground as quickly as Dr. Morgan's small stone was drawn to the meteorite.

I have one more question for the curator.

"When you were ten years old and the rock came through the window, was that when you knew you were going to move to New York City one day?"

"No, I didn't. Like your big rock up there, I had no idea where I would end up."

"Do you miss your home in Nottingham?"

"Yes, I do sometimes," the curator says.

"You can visit the meteorite anytime you want, Dr. Morgan." Then I add, "If Nana knows you're coming, she'll make fresh biscuits."

"Thank you, Henry, and I hope you and your family and your mate James will come for a tour of the meteoritic exhibition at the museum someday."

The curator stops at Nana's house and comes out with his briefcase. He hands me a small card.

MILES M. MORGAN, PHD, CURATOR
Arthur Ross Hall of Meteorites
American Museum of Natural History
212-769-5100

Underneath the phone number, there's also an email address for the curator.

"If you call, tell the operator your name and ask to be put through to me," he says.

Birdie and I watch the blue car drive over the other side of the hill. In each pocket of my coat there's a gift from the curator. In one pocket the small stone and in the other the card. By the time I think of a present I can give Dr. Morgan, the car is out of sight. If we visit the museum one day, I'll bring Dr. Morgan the M volume of the encyclopedia, with the photograph of the Ahnighito.

"Coming back?" Birdie asks me.

"I don't know. I hope one day he'll come back."

"Red tie."

"Yes, he gave you his red tie."

Birdie rubs the silky tie between her fingers, and we both stare at the empty road.

CHAPTER FIFTEEN

The water people drink today is the same water
dinosaurs drank millions of years ago.
Earth's water is about 3 billion years old.
—REBECCA OLIEN, THE WATER CYCLE AT WORK

WHEN BIRDIE AND I go back in the house, Dad has news about the water.

"The emergency-management agency says the water stopped rising but hasn't receded," he announces. "They've officially declared this section of Bower Hill Road impassable. They sank lines into the water crossing the road and measured it at twenty feet deep. Bog Road is going to be the only road to town now."

"Forever?" I ask Dad.

"Yes, it looks like the water undermined the foundations of the road, washed away the gravel and the dirt, and carved a deep stream into the earth."

"Guess the school bus is going to have to find a new route if it can't come down past here. And has the water come back to the town well?" Nana asks.

"No, not a drop. How's the water pressure here at the house?" Dad asks Nana.

Nana turns on the kitchen faucet and lets it run. As it hits the bottom of the white porcelain sink, I see flashes of green and yellow, and for a second, a quick gleam of red.

"It seems fine, same as always," Nana says.

"Can't you drill a new town well?" I ask Dad.

"It's not that easy, Henry. The aquifer is very low. Lincoln tried drilling this morning and all he got was dust. That's why we've been hauling water to town. In fact, a woman across town needs water for her animals, and I'm loaded with barrels. Come along and we'll drop them off."

Dad drives the same way Dr. Morgan did when he left, up over the hill, the only way off Bower Hill Road now. We pass Braggy in the gravel pit, dumping rocks into the rock crusher with his front-end loader. When I was little, I thought the gravel pit was like the moon—piles of rock, craters of sand, nothing growing, not even grass, in all directions. Unlike the surface of the moon, the landscape in Braggy's gravel pit is constantly changing. Braggy waves to us as we go by.

"Does Braggy like working in the gravel pit?" I ask Dad. What I really want to know is if Braggy minds not being a dowser.

"I never hear him complain about it. It keeps him pretty busy, that's for sure."

An answer that's not exactly an answer.

As we head down Main Street past the library, I see a sign tacked to a telephone pole. Written in big black capital letters on white paper are the words:

NO WATER
NO BUSINESS
NO TOWN

Dad has his eyes on the road and doesn't seem to notice the sign. Farther down the road there's another one. It says:

ASK
WHO TOOK
YOUR WATER

"Look, Dad, look at the sign."

Dad glances quickly where I point.

"What does that mean?" I ask.

"It means some people will try to lay blame wherever they can when things get rough."

Dad slows down and I wonder if he's going to stop and take down the sign. If he does, I'll tell him about the other one, but he picks up speed and turns down a dirt road. We drive up in front of a small house and a big, sagging barn.

In a fenced pasture next to the barn there's a black

pony with a white half-moon on its forehead. A woman in black barn boots hurries over to greet us. She has a long braid like Mom's but hers is dark brown.

"Thank you, Harlan." The woman looks into the bed of the truck at all the water barrels. "Dreamer will thank you, too.

"I'm Velma," the woman says to me, "and Dreamer is my horse. She drinks eight gallons of water a day, which is a lot when you're melting snow in pots on the stove. Horses need water to keep warm in the winter."

"I didn't know that," I answer. It makes me wonder what percent of water is in a horse's body.

"I heard about your house. I know how that is." Velma turns her head toward the little house next to the barn. "My parents' house got hit by lightning and burned to the ground thirty years ago. They built that house the next spring."

"I'm sorry about your old house," I say.

"That's a nice boy you have," Velma says to Dad. "I haven't seen him since he was little, the time I drove down your road and stopped at the yard sale table. Is he going to be a dowser like you and join the family well-drilling business?"

I look into the space between Velma and my father, at the big barn that leans to the left, and hold my breath, waiting for the answer.

Dad hesitates a second before he speaks.

He rolls a water barrel down a wide wooden plank onto the ground. "He's still young," he tells Velma.

I let out my breath. Another answer that's not exactly an answer. He doesn't say when *young* becomes *old enough*.

"I'll be eleven this summer," I remind him.

"That's not so young," Velma comments. "I was driving my father's team of horses when I was ten."

Velma climbs onto the tailgate and helps Dad maneuver another water barrel down the plank.

"What did you get," I ask her, "at our yard sale table?"

"I believe it was a bag of fiddleheads."

After all the barrels are unloaded and we're ready to go, Velma leans into the truck and thanks us again.

"You know, horses are picky with water, but I hear that none of the other horses around have turned up their noses at it. That's good water you have in that stream, and I'm grateful you brought it, so don't mind what people are saying."

On the drive home I think about the signs on Main Street, Miles Morgan's visit, if we will ever go to New York City, Dr. Morgan's seventeenth-floor balcony, the way the little stone moved in my pocket, the color red I'm pretty sure I saw in Nana's kitchen sink, that James is coming over tonight, if the town water will come back, the way Dad hesitated before he answered my question, how many times Braggy tried to dowse before he gave up, how long Velma's barn can stand tilted the way it is, what makes a horse be picky about water—so many things I can't give percents to how much I'm thinking about each one.

I'm so busy thinking, I don't notice at first when Dad pulls up to the gas tanks in front of the town store. Then I hear his truck door slam.

"Can I go in while you're getting gas?" I ask.

"Sure," Dad says.

I like Mr. and Mrs. Gaucher's store. I like looking at the pickled eggs in a jar, even though I wouldn't want to eat one. There are also strange things like dried pigs' ears for dogs to chew on and beef jerky for people that looks a little like the pigs' ears.

I love the chocolate and vanilla whoopie pies for sale in the front counter and how the whole store smells like the pizza they make. And it's fun to read what people tack up on the community bulletin board. Right in the middle of the bulletin board there's a poster I didn't see the last time I was there. I've never been so surprised by something on the bulletin board.

POTLUCK BENEFIT SUPPER FOR
BOWER FAMILY
WHO LOST THEIR HOUSE
IN A FLOOD
FEBRUARY 8

At the bottom of the poster it tells when the supper is and where it's being held.

"Is this a whoopie pie day for you, Henry?" Mrs. Gaucher asks me from behind the counter.

"No, I didn't bring my money. Dad's just getting gas."

Then I see a can on the counter. It's a big coffee can with a plastic top, and in the top someone cut a slit. There's a piece of paper taped around it that says,

Donations for Bower Family
Alice, Harlan, Henry, and Birdie
Lost their home in a flood

"There's a can for us?" It comes out as a question even though it's very clear what the can says. I've seen donation cans before but they've never had my name on them.

Mrs. Gaucher nods.

"Just the town pulling together," she says.

I tell Dad when I get back in the truck.

"There's a poster for a supper and a donation can for us in the store."

"Is there?" Dad says. He sounds only about twenty percent surprised. "I guess you know you're in trouble when there's a can with your name on it at the store." But he doesn't seem all that bothered by the news.

On the way home, I have one more thing to think

about—the can with our name on it at the store. There was part of a dollar sticking out on top, like someone had pushed their money in but couldn't get it down the rest of the way. How much money is in there and who are all the people who put it in?

CHAPTER SIXTEEN

A sandhill crane has a voice like no other bird.
Its call sounds like a bugle.
—Lynn M. Stone, *Sandhill Cranes*

THE MINUTE JAMES walks in the door I give him the three postcards Miles Morgan brought and tell him the whole story of the visit, from the curator's phone call to the card he gave me before the blue rental car drove out of sight.

James examines the three postcards. One is of the thirty-four-ton Ahnighito, one is of a whale swimming underwater, and one is a photo of the Museum of Natural History building.

"Maybe one day there will be a postcard of *your* meteorite," James says.

When he says that, I feel a pain in the left side of my chest. It's the same place I feel my heart beating when I run fast. The last time I had that feeling was a long time ago. It was a day Mom and I went down to the Honor Box in the morning and the table was empty. All the things from the table were scattered everywhere on the road, under the table, and in the ditch. I asked Mom if the wind had blown them off. She sat right down in the dirt then and explained that someone had stopped and knocked our things off on purpose.

She started picking them up off the ground, putting the ones that had not broken back on the table. She didn't ask me to help. Watching Mom on her hands and knees under the table, I felt that pain for the first time. I didn't know what I was feeling, but I knew it hurt.

If there was a postcard of the meteorite, it would mean the big rock got dug up and brought to live indoors in the museum in New York City, with no view of the sky it came from.

But James is watching me with his bright blue eyes so full of excitement that I answer, "Maybe there will be."

"Birdie, I'm glad you didn't want the postcards. Is that the tie Dr. Morgan gave you?" James leans across the dining room table where Birdie is sitting.

"MY tie." Birdie covers the tie with both hands so James can't touch it.

"I wasn't going to take it. I just wanted to see what it felt like. It looks very shiny."

Birdie smiles at James but keeps her hands over the tie and doesn't answer him.

"I have something to show you, too," Mom says, and holds up a metal sign with a color picture of a bird. It says ENDANGERED on the top. The bird looks like a cross between a wild turkey and a great blue heron. It's gray, with a long neck, very long legs, and a small head with a bright spot of red on the top.

"BIG BIRDS," Birdie shouts, running over to the sign.

"I think Birdie saw one of those birds when she was on top of the big rock," I tell Mom.

"They're sandhill cranes. The game warden thought he saw a flock of them the other day and came back today to check. He saw them again next to the water. Sandhill cranes are very rare and they like flooded fields. It's the perfect wetland habitat for them out there."

"What does that mean?" I ask Mom.

" 'Endangered' means people have to leave their habitat alone. They can't try to drain the field or reroute the water."

"Or shoot them," adds James, whose father hunts wild turkeys.

"Can I see?" I look at the picture on the sign. The bird's long legs and neck remind me of a dinosaur.

"So the water is good for the cranes? And people have to leave the field alone?" I ask.

"Yes," Mom answers.

"Now you have a rare rock AND a rare bird," James says.

I press the spot on my chest that still aches and think about what Mom said.

The stone brought the water, and the water attracted the sandhill cranes. Now the field is a wetland and no one can disturb it. The stone found a way to protect itself without my help, the way beavers make a moat around their lodges so foxes and coyotes can't get to them.

"I wonder if the sandhill cranes will also bring something new?"

"Yeah! Maybe a rare bug that likes to live on cranes. A crane bug!" James suggests.

James's father is working the evening shift at the mill, so James stays for supper. By the time we finish our roast chicken, mashed potatoes, and Nana's three-bean salad, it's dark outside.

Nana heads to bed early, the way she always does.

"I'm like a chicken," she tells us. "I go to bed before it's dark under the table."

Mom is on the couch again, and Dad brings her a cup of coffee. They sit there in the dark, without turning any lights on. It's just me and James and Birdie left at the table. James reads Miles Morgan's business card.

"Why don't you memorize the phone number, Henry? What if you lost the card and needed to call him? Try to memorize it and I'll test you."

I study the numbers on the business card.

2-1-2-7-6-9-5-1-0-0

Birdie takes the puzzle pieces out of the dinosaur puzzle box, one by one, and sets them on the table. She looks at each piece as she takes it out of the box and puts the colored side down.

"Birdie," James explains, "the puzzle pieces go faceup so you can see the picture, so you can see the colors. See the dinosaur on the cover."

Just as James reaches for the puzzle box cover to show Birdie the stegosaurus, the big picture window behind us bursts with a loud bang and splinters of glass shoot out everywhere. I jump out of my chair and watch James fall to the floor with a stunned look on his face, blood in his blond hair and on his shirt, and blood all around him.

My hands shake as I kneel down next to him. Cold air blows into the room through the broken window. There's a brick next to James's head with a piece of paper attached to it by a rubber band.

Birdie runs to him, screaming, "JAMES IS HURT BAD, HENRY! MAMA, COME."

James opens his eyes for a second and looks up at Birdie.

"You did it, Birdie. You said a whole sentence. And you said both of our names."

I pull the piece of paper, smeared with James's blood, off the brick, read the words on it, and stuff it down into my pants pocket.

My whole body is shaking now. James closes his eyes and doesn't move. His head lies in a circle of his own blood. I can't tell if he's breathing.

I'm frozen in place and everything happens around me.

I see Mom run full speed to the kitchen, then rush over to James. She presses a dish towel to the back of his head. Her face is next to his and she's whispering to him. Dad is on the phone giving directions. Then he lifts Birdie off the glass-covered floor and takes her down to Nana's room. He runs back and I hear him call James's father at the mill.

For the second time this week, a helicopter lands on Bower Hill Road, but this helicopter is here to take James to the hospital.

"Is he alive?" I ask the man and woman who kneel down to tend to James.

"Yes, he is." The woman wraps James's head with bandages. "But he took a big blow to the head. So it might be a while before he wakes up."

"You're sitting on glass," the man says to me, "and you're in our way. We need to move James to the stretcher."

"I don't know if I can get up. I can't feel my legs. Did you know blood is ninety-two percent water, but how can that be? This blood is so red," I hear myself saying.

"Ma'am," the man says to Mom, "this boy is in shock. He's not making sense. Can you help me lift him up and get him a blanket? He's shivering all over."

Mom and the helicopter man move me to Nana's recliner and cover me with a blanket. They roll James out the door on a bed with wheels. He'll fly in a helicopter and not even know it.

Dad brings me a cup of coffee and holds it to my lips.

"James is in good hands, Henry. There's not much more we can do right now. Take a sip."

I do, and it's so sweet it tastes like he dumped Nana's whole sugar bowl in it.

"How is Birdie? Did she step on the glass?"

"She's fine. Nana is looking after her," Dad says.

By the time I've drunk twenty-five percent of the coffee, I stop shaking. When I finish fifty percent of it, I can feel my legs again. This time it's me sitting in one place and Mom is hurrying around the room.

She cleans James's blood off the floor and searches for pieces of window glass with a flashlight. There's glass everywhere, blown far into the room, under chairs and in the cracks between the old pine floorboards. There are long, thin shards like daggers and tiny specks that catch the glow of the flashlight.

"The brick," I tell Mom, pointing to where James lay.

It looks like one of the chimney bricks that washed up next to the water where our house flooded.

Dad is outside boarding up the broken window with a piece of plywood when the policewoman comes. She's as tall as Dad and has hair the color of a hay bale. A mix of yellow and brown twisted in a knot on the back of her head. She looks very young, like the photographs of James's mother holding him when he was a baby.

She picks up the brick with plastic gloves and puts it in a plastic bag.

After she talks to Mom and Dad, she pulls a chair up to the recliner where I'm sitting and takes out a small pad and pen. She taps the pen on the pad. Rap rap rap.

"Henry, my name is Charlotte Rose and I need to ask you some questions. First, did you hear or see anything before this happened?"

I think about the night the meteorite landed in the field. How I'd first heard a rustling sound and woke up and saw the flash of light. When the brick came through the window, there was no warning at all.

"No."

"Did you look out the window afterwards?"

"No."

The policewoman is writing things down on her pad. I don't know if she's writing my answers. No. No.

"Did you hear a car or anyone walking around outside?"

"No." I try to read her notes from the recliner to see if she wrote a third no on her little pad, but her hand is in the way.

"Did anyone else see the brick come through the window?"

"My little sister, Birdie, was there. She called Mom. James had his back to the window."

"I see." The policewoman writes down something

else. Then, for the second time today, I'm handed a business card.

"Here's my card, Henry. If you remember anything else, just call me at this number. I'm sorry about your friend."

Charlotte Rose stands and shakes Mom's and Dad's hands.

"We'll get to the bottom of this. We take acts of violence very seriously," she tells them before she leaves.

When I put the business card in my pocket, I feel the note I took off the brick.

I pull it out and open it up. It's smeared with James's blood.

I read the note again.

I stare so hard at the big blocky words that when I look up at the ceiling of the room, I can see the black letters shaping themselves on Nana's white-painted ceiling.

GIVE US BACK OUR WATER

I know the note was written to me.

It was my picture in the paper next to the big rock that brought the water. I didn't even care about the reward money, as long as the meteorite was safe.

Which makes it one hundred percent my fault that James, whose mother died throwing him to safety on the ice of Eagle Lake, was hurt by a brick carrying a message meant for me. James, who stayed my best friend even though he went to school and I didn't.

I drink the rest of the too-sweet coffee. I can't fix broken glass or do anything to make James better, but when it's light out tomorrow, I'm going to find a way to give back the water.

CHAPTER SEVENTEEN

The patch of red on a sandhill's head is red skin.
Adult sandhills can be 4 to 5 feet tall.
—LYNN M. STONE, *SANDHILL CRANES*

IN THE MORNING, it's sunny out, but the plywood covering the broken window makes it dark downstairs. One of Nana's rag rugs covers the spot where James fell.

"How's James?" I ask Mom.

"Wendell called this morning. James isn't awake yet. They cleaned up the blood on the outside of his head and gave him ten stitches. But there's also bleeding inside his head."

"When do they think he'll wake up?"

"They don't know."

"If James wakes up, can you come get me?"

"Of course I will." Mom gives me a hug. The note in my pocket crinkles when she hugs me, but she doesn't seem to notice.

"Birdie, do you want to go see the big rock?" I ask her.

"James is all gone?"

"Just until he gets better," I answer.

Birdie takes my hand.

"Go see big hat."

"Wow, Birdie! You're saying lots of long sentences now!"

"Like you do, Henry." Birdie nods.

Birdie spots the sandhill cranes before I do. Two cranes are flying over the water, wide wings flapping, their long legs stretched out behind them.

"*Wahahahahah wahahahahahah.*" Birdie sings a bugle call that sounds exactly like the cranes.

"*Rahahahaha rahahahaha rahahahaha,*" the birds call back.

"Big birds talking to me," Birdie says.

"HENRY. BIRDIE. COME SEE MY NEW SIGN," Braggy yells out to us.

He's down by the moving water, standing in front of a wooden door propped against a tree. At the top of the door there are words written in orange paint.

ENDANGERED
SANDHILL CRANES
DO NOT DISTURB

Underneath the words, there's a life-sized painting of a sandhill crane. The crane is standing in the water, but its wings are stretched out like it's getting ready to fly. Braggy must have mixed colors to make the gray of the crane, because his hands are spotted black and white.

"How did you do that, Braggy? It looks just like the cranes. I didn't know you could draw."

"NEITHER DID I!" Braggy chuckles. "Not till I tried it."

"Where did you get the door, and how did you get it here? It looks really heavy."

"I took it right off my old toolshed and loaded it into the bucket of the tractor."

"Do the red hat," Birdie tells him.

"Okay, Boss," Braggy says, "I'll be right back," and he runs up the hill to the shed next to his house. He comes back with an old can of red barn paint, stirs his brush in it, and then lifts Birdie up so she can put the red on the top of the crane's head.

We all stand back and admire it. Braggy has red paint in his hair and splotches of gray paint on his boots.

"It's a very big sign, Braggy," I say.

"Not just that, Henry. Notice anything else?"

"The words are big, too?"

"Yes, but see the baling twine screwed into the bottom? I ran it all the way up to my house and connected it to a big cowbell. If anyone tries to move the sign, the bell will ring, and I'll know."

"Wow! That's a neat idea."

"The game warden hopes the cranes stay and nest here. I guess there's not many places in Maine you see sandhill cranes. Their babies are called colts. Just like horses!"

"I didn't know that. Maybe it's because they have long legs," I say.

"The game warden was very impressed with my sign. I told him his sign was too small and I'd make one myself. When James wakes up, you tell him I've got something BIG to show him."

Braggy says "when" and not "if." That makes two new things I learn about Braggy—he's an artist and an optimist.

"James will really like your painting. Are you going to sign your name on it, Braggy? I think that's what artists do."

"Good idea, Henry," Braggy says. "I don't want anyone else taking credit for it."

With the brush covered in red paint, he signs his name on the bottom.

Bragdon Bower

When the crane colts are born, they'll see the meteorite, the fast-running stream, the flooded fields, and Braggy's big door painting.

I don't have my notebook with me, but when Birdie and I get to the meteorite, I think of the questions I would write in it.

What makes you so hard?
Does your inside look the same as your outside?
How much do you weigh?
Is this place starting to feel like home?

Birdie is standing on one leg in the shallow water near the meteorite. Her other leg is tucked up behind her.

"What are you doing, Birdie?" I ask her.

She points to the flooded field. There's a sandhill crane standing very still on one foot.

"Oh, I see."

I gently touch the big rock the way I did when I first saw it, running my fingers over the silver specks and the thumbprints. The rainbow water Miles Morgan talked about hasn't completely faded—there are still faint flashes of green and yellow in the rushing stream below us.

I feel the little stone move in my pocket, as if it's being pulled toward the meteorite.

"I like the water and the cranes. I hope you're happy here," I say to the meteorite.

When Birdie and I get back to Nana's, I get the note and Charlotte Rose's card out of my pocket. I take a deep breath and make the call.

CHAPTER EIGHTEEN

*Diamond is the hardest known natural substance
on Earth. Ancient people knew no way to cut it!*
—CHRISTINE PETERSEN, *DIAMONDS*

"I THINK YOU need to start at the beginning." The policewoman, Charlotte Rose, is back at Nana's house five minutes after I call the number on her card. She taps her pen on the kitchen table and studies the note with James's dried blood on it.

GIVE US BACK OUR WATER

Mom walks past the note, but I can't tell if she sees it or not.

"First the meteorite landed. Then it started flooding the field. Then our house washed away—"

The policewoman interrupts.

"I got that part already. How about you start with this note here."

"It came in on the brick that hit James. It was tied to it with a rubber band."

She writes very quickly on her pad.

"I can't find the rubber band. Maybe it got swept up with the glass."

"Let's skip the rubber band, Henry. Then what happened?"

"I took the note because I knew it was for me."

"Yes, I know you took the note. And why did you think it was for you? I don't see your name on it." Charlotte Rose taps the note. Rap. Rap.

"I was the one who saw the meteorite fall. And the meteorite flooded the road, and then the town wells went dry."

"Those facts are true, but I still don't see why that makes the note directed at you. You didn't make the meteorite fall here, did you?"

I don't think Charlotte Rose has room on her little pad for me to explain how my dowsing stick pointed upward or how Birdie heard a *hizzzz* sound in the sky the night before the stone fell.

"I kept it secret and I made Birdie and James keep it secret, too. I didn't care about the reward. And I yelled at Mr. Ronnie to stop when he tried to chisel off a piece. He didn't know it was harder than a ten on the Mohs scale. He said people were mad because we're water witchers and we'd be sorry."

"What?" Charlotte Rose puts down her pen.

"The Mohs scale measures hardness—" I start to explain when the policewoman interrupts me again.

"Mr. Ronnie of the Picker Palace threatened you?"

"No, he just said we'd be sorry. Mom says 'sorry' can mean many things. He thinks the rock is evil."

The policewoman grabs her head with both hands.

"You're one hundred percent sure you heard Mr. Ronnie say your family would be sorry?"

I've never been asked a percent question before. What if I was only ninety-five percent sure of something? What would that mean?

Charlotte Rose taps her fingers on the table in front of me.

"Henry? Did you hear him say that or not?"

"Yes, I heard him say that. One hundred percent," I answer.

"Thank you. Is that it, or do you want to keep my card in case you think of anything else?"

"No, I told you everything."

She leans toward me.

"Are you thinking of going into police work, Henry?"

"No, I think I might study science. Or help my father and Lincoln and Braggy. Are you going to write that down?" I point to the pad.

"No. I think I've got all the information I need for now. How's your friend James?"

"He's still not awake."

The policewoman stands up.

"I'm going to take a ride by the Picker Palace."

"Will Mr. Ronnie go to jail?" I ask.

"I don't know what Mr. Ronnie has *done,* only what he's *said.* That's what I intend to find out."

She puts the note in a plastic bag and takes it with her.

I feel instantly lighter with the note gone. A piece of paper doesn't weigh very much, but it made me feel like I was walking on Jupiter. Because of Jupiter's gravity, I'd weigh two hundred and thirty-six percent more there. That would make me two hundred and twelve pounds instead of ninety.

Mom is watering her tomato seeds in their egg carton. She drips the water over her fingers into the soil a few drops at a time so she doesn't wash the seeds away. I'm glad Dad thought to bring them, because watching Mom makes me feel like I'm home again.

"I'm going to see Lincoln," I tell her.

"Yes." She says the one word like she already knows what I'm planning to do.

CHAPTER NINETEEN

Are you a dowser?
You will never know until you try.
—Joseph Baum, *The Beginner's Handbook*
of Dowsing

UNCLE LINCOLN'S HOUSE is as low and small as Braggy's is big and high. My grandfather helped him build it when Lincoln turned eighteen. Only one story—I can see into the whole house through the front-door window: kitchen, living room, bedroom, and a bathroom with a claw-foot tub like the one we used to have. Lincoln isn't inside, but there are cracking noises coming from the woodshed behind the house.

He's splitting kindling on a big stump. When he sees me, he sets the splitting axe down.

"How's James doing?"

"He's still not awake," I say.

We're both quiet then, thinking our own thoughts about James.

"Lincoln, can I ask you something?"

"Of course." He moves the wood off and sits on the splitting stump. I notice there are a few gray strands in his hair. I don't remember seeing them there before.

"Is there a way to tell if you're a water dowser?" I ask him. "Dad said it just happens."

He looks hard at me, and I wait.

"Well, it happens between you and the dowsing stick when you hold it in your hands. I think about the water." Lincoln scratches his head.

"I don't know about your father, but I feel the pull in my wrists right before the branch bends. It feels like my hands and arms are extensions of the branch. Did you ask your dad?"

"I asked him once, and he said it's not something you can teach."

Lincoln shakes his head. Words fly out of his mouth.

"It's a gift. My father and his father were some of the best dowsers around. They could find veins of water so strong a well would never run dry. That gift got passed down to your father and me."

"But not Braggy?"

Lincoln shakes his head again.

"Braggy could never get the wood to speak. He tried and tried. Tried apple wood, pear wood, even willow. Nothing. When he turned eleven, he gave up trying. It changed his nature."

"How?" I ask.

"Like he needed to prove himself. That's when he got the notion of getting his picture in the paper. I think he thought if he did that, folks wouldn't look down on him.

Not that anyone does. I don't know anyone who doesn't like Braggy."

Now I wish it had been Braggy's picture and not mine standing by the big rock in the newspaper.

"I remember he told Mom he didn't want a birthday cake for his eleventh birthday. He was that mad," Lincoln added.

"What do you think the chances are that *I'm* a dowser?" I ask Lincoln.

There's a long pause.

"The same chance as there is for anything. Fifty percent. Either you are or you aren't."

I check his face to see if he's making a joke, but his expression is serious.

An answer that's not exactly an answer.

"Once, James gave me a stick he was using to try to dowse and I think I felt it go up instead of down. I'm not sure, though. How would I find out for sure if I'm a dowser or not?"

Lincoln picks up the axe and wipes the blade with his shirtsleeve. I wait again.

"The only way to know is to try. If you concentrate on looking for water, the end of the stick will speak to you. It will pull downwards toward the water. The harder it pulls, the more water there is. You've seen that before."

"Yes, I have. How many times did you and Dad try dowsing before the stick spoke to you?"

I hold my breath, waiting for Lincoln's answer.

"For me, it happened the first time. My father had a dizzy spell and had to sit down. He handed me his stick and asked me to help. I didn't have time to think."

"And Dad?" When I let the air out of my lungs, my voice comes out in a squeak.

"The first time, your father was nerved up. He started out, then changed his mind and got back in the rig."

"And then what happened?"

"Next time was in the middle of a drought. The family had a flock of chickens just pecking around in the dust. And a new baby. Your dad cut his branch from a tree in their yard."

Lincoln stares ahead like he's seeing it all happen again. I wait.

"He found a vein so strong the chickens took a bath right there in the yard, and the folks cried themselves dry."

I tried to imagine the chickens hopping around in the water gushing out of the new well, and the family so happy they cried.

"I want to try, but I don't want Dad to know in case I can't do it. I think he'd feel bad. I have an idea and I need your help."

Lincoln is silent again, studying me closely.

"Let's hear your idea," he says.

"Okay," I say, wondering how it would be if I was like

Braggy, the son who'd been skipped over for the gift, and if it would change my nature, too. If I'd be so mad or sad I wouldn't want Nana's chocolate cake with vanilla frosting for my eleventh birthday.

It takes me a while to explain. Lincoln is good at listening. It might be his turned-out ears. He doesn't interrupt to say my idea is impossible or far-fetched. He also doesn't say it's sure to work.

"First thing tomorrow, Henry. All you can do is try. I'll come up and get you and let your dad know you're working with me."

"Thanks, Uncle Lincoln," I say, wondering what Dr. Miles Morgan would think about my plan for the little rock from Nottingham, England, and wishing James, with his optimism, could be there to see what happens.

CHAPTER TWENTY

For the maximum volume of water, you should
lay out or dowse as large an area as possible. This
is done by making a number of passes first in one
direction, and then a number of passes in another
direction perpendicular to the first series.
—Joseph Baum, *The Beginner's Handbook*
of Dowsing

THE DRILLING RIG idles at Bower One the next morning.

"I thought Henry might like coming to work with me," Lincoln tells Mom and Dad, as if it's any other drilling day when I'm going along to watch him operate the rig, not the day I'll find out whether I'm a natural-born dowser. And whether my experiment works.

I follow Lincoln outside and go over to the big apple tree in front of Nana's porch.

"Can I borrow your pocketknife?" I ask my uncle.

Lincoln gives me the knife he keeps in a pouch on his belt and looks up at the tree with me.

"This is a Baldwin apple your great-grandfather planted. They're good winter keepers, those Baldwins."

Some of the unpicked apples in the top branches hang on the leafless tree, frozen a muddy brown color. The bark on the trunk is thick and rough and has rows of small holes from sapsucker birds. The bark around the charred lightning strike is peeling off.

"It really should be pruned. Your grandfather was fussy about cutting out the suckers," Lincoln adds, looking up at the overgrown tree.

I don't need to circle the tree, because I picked my dowsing stick the day I turned ten. The branch that points toward the porch is still growing straight. The twigs that make a perfect V at the end are still even. I cut the branch about a foot above the V and show Lincoln.

"This is it. This is my stick."

Lincoln gives me a thumbs-up.

"I see. You picked it and it picked you."

I pat my pocket to be sure the stone is there. Then I climb up into the drilling rig next to Lincoln. On the way to town we drive by James's empty trailer and past fields and farms.

The other equipment is already there—the tanker truck filled with water to lubricate the drill, and the backhoe to dig a runoff ditch. That is, if the drill finds water instead of just dust and we're lucky enough to have any overflow.

Lincoln parks the drilling rig in the field next to Main Street, near the town's dry well. I jump down from the rig with my dowsing stick. There are places near us where the soil is roughed up.

"Is this where you tried drilling yesterday?" I ask Lincoln.

"Yup, got dust," Lincoln answers. "I tried three times. The stick said there was water each time, but maybe it was too deep for the drill to reach."

The field is a mix of winter and spring. Patches of frozen snow lie here and there like mini-icebergs between yellow-green tufts of grass. The sun is bright but it's cold out.

I hold the forked stick with the bottom of the Y pointing ahead and start walking, waiting for something to happen but not knowing what that something might be.

I take one small step and then another, walking in different directions the way I've seen my father and Lincoln do. I walk toward the places where they drilled and then in the opposite direction.

I walk slowly with my stick out in front of me, even with the ground. My palms hold the ends of the V.

Nothing happens.

"No hurry, take your time." Lincoln stands next to the rig, watching.

I walk over the chunks of ice frozen on the ground and through small puddles. I see the school and the library in the distance, and the backs of the stores on Main Street. I forgot my hat, and my ears hurt from the cold.

I don't feel anything. I start wondering how my nature

might change if nothing happens. I look over at Lincoln. I wait.

"It's all right, Henry. You can always try another time."

It feels like Lincoln is saying it's okay to give up, that Braggy would be happy to have company in the gravel pit when I'm older. Someone to work the rock crusher while he delivers gravel.

I turn away and keep walking. I grip the dowsing stick, but it feels like any other stick I've ever held.

I look over at Uncle Lincoln again.

"My ears are cold. I left my hat in the rig," I say to him.

Lincoln doesn't answer back, *Keep trying, I'll get your hat for you.*

Instead, he climbs into the driver's side of the rig, and while I pull my hat out from under the seat where it fell, he opens his lunch bag and passes me a piece of molasses cake wrapped in wax paper. Uncle Lincoln makes the best molasses cake. It's sticky on the outside and I lick my fingers when I'm done. He eats a piece himself, then unscrews his thermos stopper, fills the cup with coffee, and offers it to me. I take a sip. It's hot and sweet. Uncle Lincoln likes condensed milk better than sugar in his coffee, so it's a different kind of sweet than the cup Dad gave me after James got hurt.

Lincoln takes another piece of molasses cake from his bag, alternating sips of coffee with bites of the cake.

I open my door, step down, and slam it before I can change my mind.

I pick up my dowsing stick where I left it on the ground and head out into the field. I forgot my hat again, but I don't go back.

The sky is blue with clouds moving across and the wind blows in my face. I remember what Lincoln said.

I think about the water.

Huge pools of fresh water running below layers of rock. Aquifers filled with water thousands of years old.

I walk and I walk. I hear the cawing of crows and see them land in a tree behind the school, black shapes filling the bare branches. I think about what's under my feet: topsoil, sand, clay, and then the cracks in the bedrock where water flows.

Suddenly, there's a vibration in my hands. The stick is pulling me ahead, leading me. I feel a warmth in my hands and arms, like the stick is alive. The feeling gets so strong I have to grip hard to keep it between my palms and curled fingers.

I take one more step and the stick moves sharply down toward the ground.

"Stay right there!" Lincoln yells. He's leaning against the rig watching me. He runs over to where I'm standing and hammers a metal rod into the ground at the spot where the stick pointed down.

"Wow! I felt it. I really did," I tell him. "It felt like the stick was showing me where to go."

"Yes, and you paid attention," Lincoln says.

"I kept thinking about the water like you said and then it pulled right down."

Lincoln checks that the rod is secure in the ground and hammers it one more time.

"From how hard the stick went down, it could be a good vein of water, if we can reach it," he says.

There isn't anything in the book about dowsing or the book about water or the D encyclopedia that tells how it feels for the stick to come alive. I can still feel the sensation of the stick pulling me forward. I know what Lincoln meant when he said he felt like his hands and arms were extensions of the stick.

Now I also understand why Dad couldn't describe how to do it—because what happened was almost indescribable. I don't know if there's a scientific explanation, but my hands were more than hands, the stick was more than a stick. It was the most amazing feeling!

Lincoln sets up the drilling rig next to the metal rod and connects the hose from the tanker truck that lubricates the drill as it rotates and pulverizes its way down. Then he digs a ditch for the runoff. Cars pull over on Main Street, and people get out and watch.

"Okay, Henry, now's the time to try your idea." Lincoln points to the metal drill bit at the bottom of the rig.

I take Miles Morgan's little stone out of my pocket and kneel down next to the drill head. I'm so used to feeling the stone's hard little shape, I think I could recognize it with my eyes closed. I put my hand under the drill and open my fingers, and the stone flies onto the bottom of the drill the same way it did onto the big rock. Metal to metal.

Lincoln waits until I move back from the drill head before he turns on the rig. I put on the ear protectors he tosses over to me. The rig is very loud, making a constant grinding noise as the drill bores into the ground.

I've seen enough wells drilled to know what to look for. Lincoln watches to see what kind of cuttings come up around the drill. First there's dirt, then clay, the cuttings changing color the deeper the drill goes. Pipe after pipe is attached to the drill and pushed underground.

I watch.

Twenty feet.

Dirt.

Forty feet.

Clay.

Sixty feet.

Granite.

Eighty feet.

I see a small trickle of water. I can't tell if it comes from the well or from the tanker truck that's lubricating the drill. Lincoln waves and points to it, so I guess it must be coming from the well.

One hundred feet.

Water shoots out in all directions, immediately overflowing the runoff ditch. I never saw water coming so fast from a drilling site.

"It's a gusher!" Lincoln yells over the noise of the drill.

He throws his hat in the air and doesn't bother going after it. The people watching from Main Street are dancing around and shaking their hands over their heads.

"Wow!" is all I can say. "Wow!"

I wish Mom and Dad and Nana were here to see it, and Birdie, and especially James, and even Braggy.

"I'm gonna go down another twenty feet, just to be sure," Lincoln says. He attaches another pipe, and it spins round and round as it pushes down. Then he goes over to where the water is still gushing, checks his watch, watches the water fill bucket after bucket, checks his watch again, and yells, "Unbelievable! The flow rate is measuring twenty-five gallons a minute!"

"Is that a lot?"

"Most I've seen in this area is eight gallons a minute." Lincoln comes over and pats me on the back. "Looks like we got us another dowsing Bower boy in the family."

"So this will be enough for the town and the school and the car wash?"

Lincoln doesn't even pause before he answers, and he speaks as fast as I've ever heard him.

"Let's just say everyone in town can take a bath every hour of every day and there will still be more than enough water. Heck, people could go through the car wash every time they drive through town, and you'd never run dry." He adds, "While we're out here, I'm gonna put in the pump and connect it to the old pipe so people can start using it."

Lincoln attaches the rest of the metal casing and pours bentonite powder around the well to keep groundwater from leaching in. Then he caps the new well and connects it to the old pipes. Finally, he turns off the drill, lowers it to where I can reach it, and waves for me to come over.

I bend down next to the drill bit and feel for the stone the curator gave me. I remember where it attached to the bit, but all I feel now is the smoothness of the metal. I lie on my back under the drill and check all the surfaces. Nothing. The little stone is gone.

I check again and again. The stone Miles Morgan brought all the way across the ocean to New York City is gone. The pain comes in the left side of my chest again, and it's sharp, like a nail poking into me.

I shake my head at Lincoln.

"Not there?" he asks.

"Nope."

"It could've gotten broken up on the way down. But your idea surely worked."

"Yes, the water came."

Lincoln doesn't know what Dr. Morgan said about the hardness of the water rock. If a diamond can't scratch it, I don't think there's anything underground that could break up the stone. But somehow the stone found the water, or the water found the stone.

I push my fist into my chest, but it doesn't make the pain go away. The little stone that fell in Nottingham was the best gift I ever got. I liked how heavy it felt in my hand. I liked watching it fly to the meteorite. Now the stone is way down in the underground aquifer, with no way for me to ever get it back.

I rub my palms where I held the stick.

I did it, I thought, when I was ten.

I'm a dowser. And I gave back the water.

And then I think, Was it me who found the water or was it the stone? Was having it in my pocket what helped me dowse? Now that the stone is gone, if I try dowsing again, will the stick still point down to the water?

CHAPTER TWENTY-ONE

*A North American family of four
uses about 400 gallons of water in a single day.
That's enough to fill 10 bathtubs!*
—Antonia Banyard and Paula Ayer,
Water Wow!

WHEN WE GET BACK to Nana's, the house is full of people. Mrs. Kay; Mr. and Mrs. Gaucher and Fiona; the Stockfords; James's teacher, Ms. Ouellette; and some of our neighbors from Bog Road and Chicken Street. Braggy and Mom and Dad and Birdie are there, too. I can't think why everyone came to visit at the same time. It's not a holiday or anyone's birthday in the family.

There's food on the counters and the table: all kinds of casseroles, slow cookers full of beans, part of a cooked ham on a platter, and baskets of rolls. The whole stovetop is covered with pies.

"What's everyone doing here?" I ask Nana. "And where did all this food come from?"

"It's the leftovers from the potluck supper they had for your family yesterday evening. Everyone understood that your parents wanted to stay close to home after the attack on the house and James's injury, but they wanted to bring this over." Nana points to the can with our name on it in the middle of the table. "They raised four hundred and fifteen dollars!"

I peer into the can. Through the clear plastic cover and the slit on top I can see that it's filled right to the top with paper money.

Lincoln hasn't moved from the doorway. He looks as surprised to see the neighbors and food as I am.

"How did the drilling go?" Nana asks Lincoln.

"We hit the biggest gusher I've ever seen." Lincoln's usually quiet voice is raised.

It's not like Lincoln to speak up so loudly, and everyone turns to listen.

"The town has all the water it needs now."

There are cheering and clapping and foot stamping all through the room.

Lincoln holds his hand up, and everyone quiets down and waits for him to speak.

"The person you have to thank isn't me. It's HENRY here, who dowsed for the water himself."

Then the people who cheered for Lincoln come over to shake my hand, pat me on the back, and thank me. Everyone talks at once.

"Well done, Henry."

"I always knew you'd make this town proud."

"I guess like father, like son, when it comes to the dowsing gift."

I look for Dad. He's in the living room staring at me. When I go over, his eyes are wet.

"What's the matter?" I ask.

Dad rubs his eyes.

"I'm completely surprised. I had no idea you were going to try to dowse today."

"You didn't think I could do it? Is that why you never asked me to dowse?"

"Oh no." Dad clears his throat and puts an arm around me. "That's not why at all. *My* father was always talking about whether us boys had the gift. Then Lincoln did, and my father made a big fuss over it, but Braggy didn't and I worried I wouldn't, either. It was a hard thing wondering if I would let our father down, and I wasn't having *you* troubled that way."

"Would you have minded if I couldn't dowse?"

"Will you care any less about Birdie if she can't dowse?"

"No."

"There you have it. It's certainly good, but it's not everything."

"One more thing." I speak into his ear. "Before Lincoln drilled, I put the little stone that Dr. Morgan gave me on the bottom of the drill bit. I think it helped bring the water."

"I'd never have thought of that. I wish I could have seen the gusher."

I almost say I think the stone might also be what helped me find the water and I'm not a real dowser, but it feels good to have Dad's arm around me.

I check the room to see if Braggy is there. He's sitting on a folding chair next to the desserts and holding a plate with three different slices of pie. He waves to me, stands up, and addresses the group.

"No surprise to me! With Bower Brothers Well-Drilling, water is their business. When they drill, wells fill! Three generations, make that four generations now, at your service."

After his speech, Braggy sits down again and holds his plate in the air.

"Get yourself some pie, Henry. See, I'm trying the apple, the blueberry, AND the pumpkin. Don't want to hurt anyone's feelings by not choosing their pies."

Along one wall of the living room there's a stack of cardboard boxes that weren't there before I left with Lincoln this morning.

"What's in those?" I wonder out loud.

"They're for your family," Mrs. Gaucher answers. "We know you had to leave your house in a hurry, so people donated what they thought you could use. There's clothes, boots, winter coats, even some toys for Birdie in that one there." She points to a big box at the end.

The box with toys in it has a stuffed cat that's white and orange and black.

"Look, Birdie." I lift it up to show her. "Someone sent a calico cat for you."

She glances at it and shakes her head. I find another stuffed animal in the box. It's a purple parrot puppet. If James was here, he'd make the puppet say something funny, but I try my best.

"How about this one?" I put it on my hand and make the parrot's mouth open and close. "Hi there, Birdie, I'd like to be your friend."

Birdie turns her back on it.

Mrs. Kay points to one of the cardboard boxes. It's marked FOR HENRY.

"That's for you," she tells me. "Have a look. They were donated to the library years ago, and we already have a set."

In the box there are World Book encyclopedias in alphabetical order. They have black leather covers with gold letters on the bindings. The C and L volumes are missing, but all the others are there. I take out the R encyclopedia. It's stamped DISCARD on the inside.

"Thanks, Mrs. Kay. All I have from my old set is M," I say.

All around the room neighbors talk to each other.

"It's a terrible thing, hurting an innocent boy."

"As if that boy hasn't been through enough. Almost

drowned with his mother, if she hadn't been so clear-headed."

"We have a window that might fit that space."

"It's not right, the things some ignorant people are saying." Ms. Ouellette puts her hand on Mom's shoulder. "Especially with you losing your house and poor James being hurt right in front of you."

Mom reaches up and squeezes the teacher's hand. "We appreciate everything everyone's done. We're lucky in our friends and our community."

Mrs. Stockford, wearing an apron and holding a pie server, speaks to the crowd. "I want to say this. Marie's husband, Tolman"—Mrs. Stockford nods to Nana, whose name is Marie—"drilled our well for just the cost of materials back when George got sick. He was there to plow the driveway when we came home from the hospital. And he raised three good boys who help their neighbors just like he did. Alice, don't think I forgot who brought all those garden tomatoes and green beans to us when we couldn't keep a garden."

Mom waves a hand in front of herself. "That's what neighbors do," she says.

"That's right. So you let us help you now," Mr. Stockford says. "You need help building a house, Alice, we'll be there with our tools. And you tell Wendell, he needs anything when James comes home, he doesn't have to ask."

At the mention of James, some people look at me.

"What are you hearing about the boy?"

"He still hasn't woken up," Mom says. "I'm going to visit him in a bit. Wendell asked that Henry and I stop in today. He hasn't hardly left the hospital since James got hurt."

"That poor child, losing his mama so young, and now this," Mrs. Stockford says, and some people shake their heads.

Fiona gives me a big envelope. When she tucks a strand of her hair behind her ear, I notice a Big Dipper constellation on her left cheek.

"Our class made cards for James, for him to see when he wakes up. Can you bring them when you visit?"

"Sure." I take the envelope.

"You're the one who found the meteorite," she says.

"Yes, I saw it fall."

"I saw your picture in the paper. James always talked about you. He said you're his best friend. He told me you're building a stone wall. Can I see it?"

"It's underwater now."

"Sorry," Fiona says.

She sounds so genuinely sad I say, "I can build another wall sometime. There's lots of good wall-building rocks around."

"When I help my parents at the store, I carry boxes of groceries out to people's cars. Some of them are really heavy. So I can definitely move rocks around. Let me know when you start."

"Sure, it goes faster with two," I answer.

"Are you going to have some pie, like your uncle said?"

I realize how hungry I am after being outside in the cold all morning.

"Okay."

"We brought the pumpkin. You should try it, it's really good."

Fiona cuts a piece of the pumpkin pie and hands it to me on a plate. Her hair is almost the same orange color as the pie. She watches while I take a small bite.

"It's very good. Very pumpkiny," I say.

"I don't think that's a word. Pumpkiny," she says.

"You just said it," I point out.

"That doesn't make it a word."

"Anyway, I like your pie. It's very good."

"I know. So how come you're homeschooled?"

"My mom says I can learn whatever I want to right here. But each year I get to choose—home or school."

"Are you ever going to choose school?"

"My sister might miss me if I was gone all day."

Birdie is swinging in her swing in the living room, still wearing the red tie. And I realize I just gave Fiona an answer that's not really an answer.

"She's sweet." Fiona waves at Birdie. "Did you know that all the seventh graders at school are getting their own laptop this fall? For free. All the seventh graders in Maine can get one."

"I didn't know that," I said. "If I had a laptop, I could

email the curator of the science museum. He came to see the rock and gave me his business card."

"You probably could, if you wanted to. Oh, and I heard about your house. I'm sorry it got flooded," Fiona says.

"Thanks. The meteorite is safe where it is, though. Do you want to see it sometime?"

"Yes!"

I see Mom getting her coat on.

"I have to go. Thanks for the pie suggestion," I say to Fiona, and hurry into the kitchen. I find one of Nana's small canning jars and run the tap. If you didn't know to look for them, you could hardly see the colors anymore. Maybe whatever minerals the rock pulled out of the earth are almost gone. I hope there's enough left of whatever cured Miles Morgan and fixed Nana's knees.

I wait until I see flashes of green and yellow, put the jar underneath just in time to catch them, and seal the lid tight.

CHAPTER TWENTY-TWO

*The Clackamas Indians held the meteorite
to be a sacred object and believed that a union
occurred of the earth, sky and water when it
rested in the ground and rainwater collected
in its many folds and basins.*
—THE NEW YORK TIMES, JUNE 23, 2000

JAMES HAS HIS own room in the hospital, and one wall is all glass. In the glass wall, there's a glass door, and a nurse slides the glass door open for me and Mom to come in. James's dad, Wendell, is standing behind the glass door.

If you saw Wendell and James together, you'd know right away that they were related. Wendell's hair is not as blond as James's, but his eyes are the same bright blue. Today he looks like he forgot to pack a comb and a razor when he left for the hospital, because his hair sticks out on top and I don't think he's shaved in a while. He smiles when he sees us and gives Mom a hug.

"It's darn good to see you. It's all strangers in this place," Wendell says.

"It's good to see you, too," Mom answers, "and to see your boy."

"Your boy, too. We both know how James feels about you and your family. And I couldn't keep doing shift work at the mill without your being there for him." Wendell glances behind him where James lies. "If you don't mind, I'll get myself some lunch down in the cafeteria while you're here. I hate to leave him alone, even if he's not awake."

"Take your time," Mom says. "We'll be here."

Wendell lets himself out of the glass wall, and Mom sits down on a stool next to James's bed.

First, I look at everything in the room except James, who lies there as still as he did on Nana's floor.

At the bottom of the bed there are square buttons with up and down arrows that say HEAD HEAD BED BED FOOT FOOT.

There are things attached to the wall over James's head that look like they're made from old plumbing parts. I can't even guess what they're used for. Plastic bags with coils of plastic tubing are hooked to the bed. It reminds me of the tubing the big maple syrup farms loop through the woods in spring. There's a helium balloon floating below the ceiling that says GET WELL. I wonder if James's school friends sent it. I put the envelope Fiona gave me on a nightstand next to James's bed so he'll see it when he wakes up.

James's room has a bathroom attached to it. The door is partly open and I can see a sink and a toilet but no shower.

I'm running out of things to look at in James's room when Mom starts singing a song I remember from when I was little.

> The barn swallow roosts
> on the rafters.
> The deer beds down
> in the pines.
> And what about you,
> my child,
> where do you rest
> when darkness comes?

A nurse brings in more plastic tubing and I watch him move around James's bed.

"I don't see anything for James to drink," I whisper.

"James can't drink just yet. See this?" The nurse shows me a plastic cup half filled with water and what looks like a toothbrush with a pink sponge on the end. "We wet his mouth with it."

When the nurse leaves the room, I take the plastic cup into the little windowless bathroom. I close the door behind me, pour the water down the sink drain, and quickly refill the cup with water from the canning jar in my coat pocket. When I hold it up to the mirror over the sink, I see a swirl of bright green that disappears as quickly as a green garter snake in tall grass.

I go to the opposite side of the bed from Mom and stand near James. Except for a bandage on his head, and the fact that his eyes are closed, he looks the same. Same short blond hair and same light eyebrows. The white bandage has brownish-red spots on it.

I swish the pink sponge round and round in the water in the cup. With my back to the glass wall, in case the nurse looks in, I squeeze the sponge over James's lips. I squeeze it again and again, trying to make the water go in James's mouth and not drip down his chin. Mom watches but doesn't say anything. She keeps singing, holding James's hand in hers.

> *The honeybee sleeps*
> *in the flower,*
> *the spider hangs*
> *from its web.*
> *And what about you,*
> *my child,*
> *where do you rest*
> *when darkness comes?*

When Mom stops singing, I lean over and speak in James's ear.

"If you can hear me, James, I have an idea. Our road ends in a deep stream now, so there's no use putting out the Honor Box table. Nobody will drive past anymore. I was thinking, since everyone has to go by you on Bog Road now, we could set up the Honor Box at the end of your driveway. You could sell stuff you find and Mom and I could bring our things there, too."

James doesn't move. His chest breathes up and down and his eyes stay shut. Wendell comes back and Mom stands at the glass door talking to him.

While they're busy talking, I take what's left of the water in the cup and pour it over the bandage on James's head.

"I'm sorry, James," I whisper, shaking the cup upside down so the last few drops come out on the stained bandage.

It's dark when we leave the hospital. I look up at the windows, trying to figure out which one is James's. We rode the elevator to the third floor and then went down two long halls. All the windows on the third floor are lit up, and they're all the same size. I wish I'd taped something to James's window so I could recognize it from outside.

Mom drives down Bower Hill Road, but instead of turning into Nana's driveway, she keeps going until we reach the concrete barricades blocking the road. She turns the car off and opens the window. We can hear the water streaming down the hill.

"Why did you come here?" I ask her.

"Let's just watch the water a minute."

"But it's dark out," I say.

"Yes, it's almost the new moon. Give your eyes time."

As my eyes adjust to the dark, I see the faint sliver of the moon above the water where our house used to be. In the marshy field I see the silhouettes of birds, their long, thin legs like sticks holding up their big bodies. Their necks are long, too, and their beaks are pointy. I count each tall shape.

"There's fifteen cranes," I tell Mom.

"They love the water," she says.

"The water is losing its color."

"I thought so."

"Why did you sing James a lullaby if he was already asleep?"

"I don't know. Just the song that came to me when I saw him."

"That girl Fiona asked me if I was going to go to school. She's in James's class."

"It's up to you. Wherever you are, you won't stop learning."

"People are saying they'll help us build a new house. Are we going to build a new house?"

"Do you want us to build a new house?" Mom asks me.

"At first I did. But I'm getting used to Dad and Braggy's old room. I like how quiet it is when the door is closed. And Birdie has her swing in the living room."

"Okay, then," Mom says.

"Did the collector call about the meteorite?"

"He did. Your father took the call the other day."

"Did Dad tell him the meteorite is too hard to cut into? Does he want to buy the whole thing?"

"I didn't hear him talk about how hard it is. But I did hear your father say that some things aren't for sale."

It's too dark to see the meteorite in the corner of the field, but I'm sure if I had to, I could find my way to the rock without a flashlight. Ever since it fell, I've kept its position fixed in my mind, like old sailors used the North Star.

"Are you glad I can dowse, like Dad and his father?" I ask Mom.

"If you are."

That sounds like both a question *and* an answer.

"Yes. It was amazing feeling my stick move, and I'm happy we got the water back for the town. But I'm not sure I could do it again. I think the little stone Dr. Morgan gave me was what helped me dowse."

"You know that's not the only gift you have, Henry," Mom says.

"No?" I don't know what other gift she means.

"You see the world with your own eyes, and you're kind to your sister."

I don't think those are gifts. Everyone uses their own eyes to see the world, and who wouldn't be kind to Birdie?

Suddenly the cranes take flight, their big wings

flapping, their long legs trailing behind. We hear their loud, trumpeting calls.

"Guess it's time for us to go home, too," Mom says.

When we get back to Nana's, supper is all the food neighbors and friends brought for us. Everything tastes a little bit the same and a little bit different. I'm used to Nana's baked beans. These have some kind of spice that's good but makes my tongue burn. The macaroni and cheese has orange cheese instead of yellow like Mom's. The Jell-O salad has whipped cream, but the whipped cream is mixed inside the Jell-O, not scooped on top.

Dad takes a bite of the beans, then a drink of water, a bite of beans, then another drink of water.

"I'm tasting those chili peppers Darlene grows," Dad says between sips.

"The mac and cheese is kinda cheery, so bright like this," Mom compliments the dish.

I serve myself some of the Jell-O salad, green and white swirled together in a round bowl, and it's much better than I expect.

"Do you want to try some of this, Birdie? It's really good." I hold up another spoonful.

"No, Henry. I eat pie."

Birdie's plate has a slice of Fiona's pumpkin pie and a slice of blueberry pie.

There's new glass where the window broke, and I hear the call of a barred owl far off in the woods. I decide

Nana's house is like the food we got. It's different than the house we lost, but also the same. My view out the window in the upstairs room is in the same direction as my old bedroom. I can still see the sun rise in the morning. Only now, instead of a view of the field, I see a stream shimmering with reflected light. It's not the same, but it's good.

CHAPTER TWENTY-THREE

American Indians . . . have treated rivers with the greatest awe. Some tribes believed that fast-flowing springs were sacred and that the bubbles that issued from them were caused by the breathing of spirits.
—FRED POWLEDGE, *WATER*

THE NEXT DAY I wait. I wait to hear what Charlotte Rose finds out about Mr. Ronnie. I wait to hear how James is doing. Every minute feels like an hour. Every hour feels like a month. Especially since I don't know if what I'm waiting for will be good news or bad.

While I'm waiting, the doorbell rings. It's Mr. Ward from the Lowington Fire Department with a bag of mittens, hats, gloves, and scarves. There are small ones for Birdie, ones that fit me, and bigger sizes for Mom and Dad.

The phone rings, too. News has spread about the gusher, and there are calls from people who want me to dowse a well for them. I write down their names and numbers.

"Come for a walk with me, Henry," Nana says after one of the phone calls. "Take your mind off things for a bit."

We go over the hill past the gravel pit, and Nana stops to look at the quarry. It's a deep hole cut in the side of the hill, with huge slabs of speckled granite sticking out from the dirt.

"Your grandfather quarried the granite foundation for our house from here. And most of the granite for the county courthouse and the town library came out of this quarry."

Nana always stops here and tells me this same story. I listen to be polite, but today I look at the hole and try to imagine what it was like when my grandfather worked the stone.

"Really? How much granite is in there?" I ask her.

"More granite than you could cut in your lifetime. The boys got busy with drilling and selling gravel from the pit and let the quarry go. Why, do you think you might want to get it going again someday?" Nana's winter coat is buttoned up to her neck, and her hat is pulled down over her ears. Only a little bit of white hair sticks out in the back.

"I don't know. I like rocks."

My hand feels in my pants pocket out of habit, reaching for the little stone, before I remember it's gone.

"It's a real art, cutting stone. You have to be patient and follow the lines in the granite, your grandfather used to say."

When Nana and I walk back down the hill, there's a car I don't recognize in the driveway. It's bright orange.

Charlotte Rose is sitting in the driver's seat and waves at me to come over.

I get in the front seat. Her long hay-colored hair is tied back in a ponytail. She taps her fingers on the steering wheel. When she turns to talk to me, I notice for the first time that she has mossy eyes like Mom and Birdie and me.

It takes a long time for her to explain what happened. When she's done, she asks if I want to go with her.

"Your parents are willing to let you go. Mr. Ronnie really wants to see you, but it's up to you."

"Yes, but you're sure it wasn't Mr. Ronnie who threw the brick?"

Charlotte Rose already said that, but I want to be very sure. One hundred percent sure.

"No, he didn't. He'll tell you himself."

She starts the car, and the radio comes on at the same time. We head up Bower Hill toward town.

"You're not going to arrest him?"

"Do I look like I'm going to arrest anyone? No police car, no uniform, no handcuffs. This is going to be a friendly visit."

Charlotte Rose has a plastic troll with orange hair hanging from the rearview mirror on a chain.

"Mr. Ronnie tried to take a piece of the meteorite," I remind her.

"I know. He's not going to be trying *that* again. By the way, what's happening with your space rock? I heard you turned down that reward but now some bigwig scientist from New York City is interested in taking it."

"He's interested IN it, not in TAKING it," I explain.

We pass the 25 mph speed limit sign in town, and the speedometer pointer goes to 40 mph as we round the corner. Charlotte Rose pulls up in front of Mr. Ronnie's store.

The Picker Palace hasn't changed at all since the last time I was in there. It might even be more crowded. There's only room enough to walk one in front of the other toward the back of the store. I follow Charlotte Rose. The piles start on the floor and go almost to the ceiling. Stacks of books, buckets of tools, chairs on top of tables, birdcages, huge spools of rope, old lawn mowers, tire rims, pitchforks, lamps, strips of sheet metal, and rusted sewing machines. There are more things piled behind the stacks we walk past, but I can't figure out how anyone would get to them. The Picker Palace is like an iceberg. You can only see about ten percent of what's there.

All the way in the back, the narrow path through the store opens to a small clearing, where Mr. Ronnie stands. There's no space to even set a chair. The black-and-white dog lies under a table.

Charlotte Rose puts her arm around my shoulders and speaks to Mr. Ronnie.

"Henry is best friends with James, and he was there during the assault. He's willing to hear what you have to say."

Mr. Ronnie wears his green-and-black-plaid jacket. It's cold in the store, almost as cold as it is outside. His head is bent and he talks into the collar of his jacket.

"The Palace's not been doing too good. I lost my house and moved in upstairs here. I thought if I could get the reward for a piece of that rock it would help. I didn't see you folks lining up to get the money. My son, Dwayne, was mad I lost our house and wanted me to sell this building and give him half the money so he could buy himself a piece of land. But who'd buy it without water?"

When Mr. Ronnie says his son's name, the dog picks his head up and barks once.

"Quiet down, Badger," Mr. Ronnie tells the dog. "He's not coming back anytime soon."

The dog puts his head back down on the dusty floor, and Mr. Ronnie continues with his story.

"I got Dwayne riled up about the rock and the water. Told him it was the rock's fault and your father's fault for witching away our water. We never had a flood or a drought like this before and I lived in Lowington my whole life. Never had a space rock fall out of the sky. Yes, I did put up those signs in town. It's not against the law to say what you think. I know Dwayne has a short fuse, but I didn't think he'd do anything like throwing a brick through your window and hurting that boy so bad. He was in jail before for fighting, but this time he's gonna be there a long time."

Mr. Ronnie looks up at us then.

"Dowsers don't take away water, they find it. And now there's a new well that has lots of water," I explain.

"Yes, I know, and I heard tell it was you yourself found the water, when no one else could." Mr. Ronnie holds up a mug full of water. "Good-tasting water it is, too."

Charlotte Rose taps her fingers on a metal toolbox in front of her.

"Mr. Ronnie, I think we're getting a bit off the subject. Did you say what you needed to say?"

"I'm sorry. I'm sorry and I hope your friend gets better and comes home. That's what I meant to say, but maybe it didn't come out clear."

"It was clear," I answer.

"Good. Now that's done. Son, I want you to pick out something. Anything from the whole Palace."

I've been looking around, so it isn't hard to choose. I see a wooden apple ladder that comes to a point at the top. With the tall ladder, I can pick the apples that get left at the top of my great-grandfather's tree every fall. And in the winter, I can ask Dad to show me how to prune the high-up suckers.

It takes a while for Mr. Ronnie to reach the ladder and bring it outside.

"Might you have a piece of rope to tie this ladder to the top of my car?" Charlotte Rose asks Mr. Ronnie.

"A piece of rope? I have miles of rope! That's not a problem at all."

Mr. Ronnie helps Charlotte Rose tie down the ladder.

Then he goes back into the store and comes out with a big doll. It has stains on its yellow flowered dress and blue Magic Marker on its bald head.

"Here, take this for that little sister of yours. What's her name? Tweety?"

"Birdie."

"Yes, you give this to Birdie from me. So she doesn't feel left out."

Mr. Ronnie sticks his hand out.

"No hard feelings?"

"No hard feelings," I say, and shake Mr. Ronnie's hand. "I hope you don't have to sell the Picker Palace. There's some great things in here."

"Thank you, son."

It's a short ride home with Charlotte Rose. The rock music plays, and I think about Mr. Ronnie's son, Dwayne, in jail. I guess that would be the worst thing, to be where you can't smell the spring or see the stars at night. I'm glad the meteorite found a way to protect itself and be outdoors under the sky.

Mr. Ronnie's spools of rope give me an idea for measuring the distance around the meteorite using hay string. I picture myself holding one end of the string and James stretching it out all around the rock. Then I remember where James is.

Birdie runs at me when Charlotte Rose drops me back at Nana's.

"Where you go, Henry?"

"To town. Mr. Ronnie sent this for you," I say, and show Birdie the doll.

"Oh! Sweet dirty baby." Birdie grabs the baby doll and hugs it to her chest, then throws it across the room into the kitchen sink. "I clean you up."

CHAPTER TWENTY-FOUR

*Most granite once was hotter than lava, but it
cooled and hardened deep underground.*
—CARROLL LANE FENTON AND
MILDRED ADAMS FENTON, *ROCKS AND THEIR STORIES*

I go up to my room and open my notebook.

What makes a quarry?
How did the granite get on Bower Hill?
How do you follow the lines in the
granite?

The pages of the Q encyclopedia Mrs. Kay gave me
smell like the inside of Nana's old wooden trunk, and
pressed between some of them are dried leaves. I turn
the brittle pages carefully until I find what I'm looking
for. I'm concentrating so hard I don't notice at first when
Fiona comes into the room.

"You're reading the encyclopedia? Who reads the encyclopedia?"

Fiona's dark brown eyes are curious and puzzled at
the same time.

"*I* do. Not the whole encyclopedia. Just volume Q." I hold up the heavy book.

"That's a very old book." Fiona comes over and traces the gold letter Q on the black spine. "My mother and I dropped off a casserole, so I thought I'd come say hi. I didn't know you could read," she teases.

"I can read. What kind of casserole?"

"Noodles and peas and mushrooms, mostly. It sounds strange but it's really good."

"Mushroomy," I say.

"Yes, definitely mushroomy. What are you reading about? Quicksand? Quiches?"

We both laugh at that.

"Granite quarries. We have one on the other side of the hill. I just read that granite rock used to be molten lava."

Fiona sits down next to me on the floor, and I turn the encyclopedia so she can see the photo of the Rock of Ages granite quarry in Vermont. The picture is in black-and-white, but it says the water at the bottom of the quarry is green.

She looks at the photo, and then she notices my notebook on the floor. "Henry Ten. What does that mean?"

"It's my homeschool notebook. I get one every year on my birthday. I can write, too."

Fiona laughs.

"We had to keep a notebook in English last year. With

a list of all the books we read and what we thought of them. Is that what's in your notebook?"

"No, it's mostly questions. About science or experiments I'm thinking of doing."

"I got an A-minus on my notebook. The minus 'cause I write sloppy. What about you? What grades do you get?"

"No one looks in my notebook. It's just for me. I don't get grades. How sloppy do you write?"

"So sloppy the teacher can't read it. You don't believe me? Give me a pen and I'll show you." Fiona sounds proud to write so sloppy a teacher can't read it.

"I only have a pencil." I give her my pencil.

Fiona turns the pages. "It's more than half full."

"I'll be eleven in August."

She finds a blank page near the back and writes for a while. I watch her write. No one else has ever written in my notebooks. When she's finished, she passes the notebook to me. She writes in cursive, but the loops and curves on the letters get bigger and bigger each sentence she writes.

"See, the more I write the sloppier it gets."

"I wonder why. You could do an experiment. Like stop after every sentence and see what happens. Or print instead of cursive."

"Print is worse. We do experiments in school. In science last year we made sedimentary rock in milk containers. In all these layers. It was really fun."

"We have a big outcrop of sedimentary rock in the family cemetery. I'll show you sometime, if you want."

"You have your own cemetery?"

There's a sudden noise on the stairs behind us as Birdie jumps her way up from one step to the other, shouting as she jumps, "I CAN KEEP A SECRET. I CAN KEEP A SECRET."

"Hi, Birdie," Fiona says.

"Hi, I can keep a secret."

"That's good."

"Mom says come down," Birdie tells us.

"Now?"

"YES. I can keep a secret."

"Okay."

Birdie leads the way downstairs, holding on to the railing, as she calls out, "I DIDN'T TELL. I DIDN'T TELL. I DIDN'T TELL."

Birdie can hardly contain herself as she runs into the kitchen.

"SEE!" she yells, pointing.

I can't believe my eyes.

James is sitting at the kitchen table, in the same seat he sat in when the brick came through the window. Wendell is there, too. James doesn't have a bandage on his head, but when he turns to look at us, I see that part of his hair in back is missing.

Seeing James in Nana's house again feels like watching

the fireball light up the field. It's completely unexpected and amazing.

"JAMES! JAMES!" I yell louder than Birdie. "You're back!"

"I can't wait to tell everyone at school." Fiona claps her hands.

"Why are you all up here at Nana's house?" James asks, looking from me to Mom to Wendell to Birdie to Fiona.

"The water flooded our house, remember? We live up here now," I say.

Wendell holds up a hand. "James doesn't remember everything that happened before the, you know . . ."

"Don't fall on the floor," Birdie tells James.

"What?" James looks even more confused.

Wendell shakes his head at us from behind James.

"Birdie said your name and mine, James," I say. "And she said it in a whole sentence."

"I said James," Birdie agrees.

"Wow, Birdie! That's great!" James smiles, and in that moment, he looks like the old James.

"Why aren't you at *your* house, Henry?" James says again.

"We're staying with Nana now. I'm sorry you got hurt, James," I say. "How does your head feel?"

James touches the back of his head.

"I got stitches. But they don't hurt at all. The nurses

said they would itch, but they feel fine. I had a funny dream. I dreamt you told me I could have the Honor Box and we could set it up in front of our trailer."

"That wasn't a dream. I visited you in the hospital and told you that."

I get the wooden Honor Box down from the mantel and give it to James.

"Here. I'll help you set up the table if you want. Whenever you're ready."

"That shouldn't be too long," Wendell says. "The doctors are surprised how quickly he woke up and how much better he is. A few hours after you and your mom visited, James opened his eyes. The nurses said it was a real miracle."

"When are you going back to school?" Fiona asks him.

"I don't know," James says. "What happened to me?"

"You got hurt, but you're getting better." Wendell steers James toward the door. "Let's head home now, James. It's only your first day out of the hospital."

"How's your rock doing?" James asks me.

"Good. I'll tell you all about it next time you come. There's a lot to tell. But it's safe there in the field. I also went drilling with Lincoln and he let me do the dowsing."

"I always knew you were a dowser," James says, even though I didn't tell him how the dowsing turned out.

On his way out, James gives Mom a hug.

"I think you sang to me," he says.

"You're right. I did." Mom hugs him back.

"I remember."

James stops in the doorway. With a hat over the shaved part of his head, you can't tell that he was hurt.

He might not remember everything, but he remembers the Honor Box and Mom's singing and the big rock. He's different and the same.

"It's good you're at the top of the hill now," James says. "The wind is really strong up here and that'll blow the mosquitos away."

I watch James walk out the door. I think Miles Morgan would be very happy to hear that even though he got hit by a brick, James is still an optimist.

CHAPTER TWENTY-FIVE

You must face up to the fact that dowsing will put a strain on your ability to admit and accept what you can do and will soon be doing. At the same time you must be prepared to treat this faculty of dowsing with respect and always make use of it in a responsible manner.
—RAYMOND C. WILLEY, *MODERN DOWSING: THE DOWSER'S HANDBOOK*

"VELMA CALLED. She wants a new well drilled. Lincoln and I are headed there this morning," Dad says at breakfast.

He's making ployes on Nana's cookstove. The wind must have blown the ploye smell down the hill, because Braggy shows up just in time to try the first ones out of the cast-iron skillet. Lincoln is down by the water, filling up the tanker truck.

Nana opens the jar of maple syrup James rescued from the house before it flooded and dribbles it over Birdie's ployes. Since her high chair got washed away, Birdie sits in a regular chair. She's propped up on the X and Z encyclopedias from the box Mrs. Kay gave me.

James would have come for breakfast, too, but he has to see the doctor today and get his stitches out.

When Dad says that about drilling a well for Velma, I know what I need to do.

Ever since I dowsed the town's water and lost the little stone from Miles Morgan, I keep thinking,

I'm a dowser.

No, I'm not, not really.

I gave the water back.

No, it was the stone that did it, not me.

"Can I do the dowsing for Velma's well?" I ask Dad.

Braggy looks up from his ployes when I say that.

"If you want to. I don't see why not." Dad nods.

"Great! She's the lady with the pony named Dreamer, right?" I remember the day we unloaded the barrels of water and saw the black pony and the tilted barn.

"I go see the pony, too." Birdie bounces on the encyclopedias.

"Birdie, sweetie." Mom smooths Birdie's hair. "Dad and Lincoln can't watch you when they're drilling."

"I pet the pony." Birdie lifts her hand and shows us how she'd do it.

"I'll take you, Birdie," Braggy says. "You and I can pet the pony while these guys do all the work."

"You can pet, too," Birdie agrees.

"Was it the big rock that made Velma's well go dry?" I ask.

"No, she's had trouble with water for a long time," Dad says. "She used to haul it from the town well. Her land sits on ledge and all she has is a dug well."

A dug well is a lot cheaper than a drilled well. All you need is a shovel and plenty of time, or someone with a backhoe. But a backhoe and a shovel can't dig through ledge because ledge is solid bedrock that's under the dirt and you don't know it's there until you hit it. You could hit it at five feet or fifteen feet and that's how deep your dug well will be.

An hour later five Bowers pull into Velma's driveway in three different vehicles—me and Dad in the drilling rig, Lincoln in the tanker truck, and Braggy and Birdie following behind in his pickup. If I can't find water, there will be six people, including Velma, to see it.

It's like Lincoln said, it's fifty percent whether I can or I can't, but even if I can't I'll still be one hundred percent Henry.

Now I also know you can't explain everything with percents.

You can't measure the percents for all the great things that happened after the rock from space fell in our hayfield—the sandhill cranes, meeting Miles Morgan, Braggy finding out he's an artist, bringing back the water. Even getting to know Fiona and Mr. Ronnie and Velma. Then the bad things—losing our house, the town well drying up, James getting hurt, Dwayne going to jail.

The other thing I figured out—good things can make bad things happen, and bad things can cause good things. You can't calculate percents for how that works, either.

When we pull into the driveway, the black pony with the white half-moon on her forehead gallops over to the pasture fence. Velma waves to us. She's wearing the same black barn boots, but her brown hair is loose instead of in a braid. A yellow puppy runs next to her.

Where the tilted barn used to be is a pile of criss-crossed boards and beams. I roll down my window and lean my head out. Velma sees where I'm looking.

"Yup. The barn finally collapsed. Half a foot of wet snow did her in."

"Wow!" I say. I try to imagine the sound the barn made when it fell.

"I'll rebuild in the spring. Just a small barn with one stall and a feed area."

Velma taps the dowsing stick I'm holding. I cut another perfect branch from Nana's tree before we left.

"You're going to dowse my new well, Henry?" she asks.

"I hope so."

The dog runs around Velma's legs.

"I didn't know you had a puppy," I say.

"I just got him. He's good company for Dreamer, and for me, too. Even if he chews everything in sight."

Velma goes over to Lincoln and Braggy and Birdie.

Birdie sits down in the snow and lets the yellow puppy lick her face.

I turn to Dad.

"I might not be a dowser," I warn him. "It could have been Dr. Morgan's little stone that helped me find it last time."

"That's okay, Henry."

I jump down from the rig. My boots make footprints in the snow as I walk across Velma's front lawn.

"Didn't the boy bring a hat?" I hear Velma say.

"He dowsed bareheaded last time, too," Lincoln tells her. He and Dad follow me. Lincoln carries the steel rod and a hammer.

The dowsing stick feels familiar in my hands. The forks of the V rest in my upturned palms, and the long end points ahead. I grip the forks enough to feel the wood, but I don't clench my fingers around them like last time. It will happen or it won't.

Think of the water, Lincoln said.

I don't know if the stick is leading me or I'm guiding the stick, but I find myself walking across the snow to the back of Velma's house like I'm being pulled by an invisible magnet.

There's a row of sunflower stalks, corn stubble, and wooden stakes sticking out from a square that must be Velma's kitchen garden. Next to it stands a trellis of grapevines.

Suddenly, like the last time I dowsed, there's a vibration and a warmth in my hands.

I slow my steps, and the stick bends down just past the trellis.

I look up. Dad and Lincoln are both smiling. With three big whacks of his hammer, Lincoln pounds the rod into the ground in the place where the stick pointed.

"Time to go to work," Dad says, "and see if we can get that pony some water."

CHAPTER TWENTY-SIX

It is known to often pass from grandfather to grandson, from mother to son, from father to daughter. As many women can dowse as men.
—RAYMOND C. WILLEY, *MODERN DOWSING: THE DOWSER'S HANDBOOK*

BIRDIE AND BRAGGY and Velma are in the pasture. Dreamer has her head bent down and Birdie is petting her nose. The puppy is lying next to Birdie's feet.

"Braggy," Velma says, "I've seen some of your paintings. When I get my new barn built, will you paint a picture of Dreamer on her stall door? I'm not sure what you charge, but maybe I could pay you off over time."

"Sure. I'm not worried about getting paid," Braggy answers. "I know you have HORSE SENSE. C-E-N-T-S."

"Pet the pony, Henry," Birdie says.

"Yes, I see you're petting her."

"YOU pet her, Henry."

I stroke Dreamer's mane. It's rougher than I expect, like the unraveled ends of a rope.

Dad and Lincoln start up the rig and the tanker truck and drive behind the house.

Birdie reaches for my dowsing stick.

"I do it, too. Like you."

She holds the ends of the V in her hands and walks across Velma's lawn in the same direction I did. The yellow puppy runs along next to her. I can't tell if Birdie's following my footprints or if the stick is leading her the way it did for me.

She heads around the house toward Velma's garden, then stops.

"It's shaking me." Birdie laughs and throws the stick in the air. When it lands, the puppy runs over and picks it up in his mouth.

Did Birdie feel the vibrations like I did?

Would the dowsing branch have led her to the same spot it led me to?

Dad backs the rig up to the spot where the stick bent. The pounding begins as the drill rotates its way into the ground, pulverizing the rock. Dad adds drill rod after drill rod and Lincoln pumps in water from the tanker truck.

Birdie chases after the puppy, grabs the stick back, and throws it again.

All I see coming up is clay dust.

Velma calls to us.

"Henry and Birdie, come inside and warm up. You can watch the progress from my back window. It may take a while for them to get through the ledge. I'm heating up apple cider for your uncle Braggy, if you'd like some."

"I drink apple cider," Birdie says. "Come, puppy."

The puppy follows Birdie and me into the house with the stick in his mouth.

Velma is right. There's a window that looks out on the garden and the trellis. I never sat in someone's house and drank hot cider while I watched Dad and Lincoln drill. Especially not for a well I dowsed myself. It isn't as noisy as it was outside. I can hear Birdie blowing on her cider and taking little sips. Braggy drinks his cider and narrates what's happening outside like we're watching a movie.

"That drill is going through bedrock like butter."

"Don't look away. We're gonna see water coming anytime now."

When the water does come, I'm not looking out the window. I'm drinking my cider and watching the puppy, who's lying under a table chewing up my dowsing stick. It's funny because he acts so excited about the stick, but the more he plays with it, the shorter it gets. I don't mind, because I'm done with it. I'll need a fresh green branch the next time I dowse.

Braggy hollers, "Get your water jugs, get your buckets, get your bathing suits!"

It's not a gusher, but clear water steadily pumps out into the runoff ditch.

Velma claps her hands.

"I never thought I'd see the day! It's going to be so easy to water Dreamer now."

"That depends," Braggy says. "You can lead a horse to water but you can't make 'em drink."

Velma laughs at Braggy's joke, then comes over and gives me a hug.

"Thank you, Henry, for finding the water. I really appreciate it. When your father and uncle get the line connected to the house, I'm going to spend a week in the bathtub."

I think Braggy's exaggerating is rubbing off on Velma, but I don't say that. Braggy could be right that if you look at things a certain way, they seem bigger. After all, if a millions-of-years-old rock lands in your hayfield, how could you ever think the world was small?

"You're welcome," I answer, and go outside. I want to see it up close and put my fingers in the second water I dowsed for.

CHAPTER TWENTY-SEVEN

Meteorites are not cut into thin segments just to make them more beautiful, however. Scientists often remove small pieces of meteorites to distribute this rare research material among many laboratories, ensuring wide access to the samples. In addition, nearly all scientifically important characteristics can be seen best by cutting into meteorites.
—AMERICAN MUSEUM OF NATURAL HISTORY, NEW YORK CITY

IT'S FORTY SUNRISES and forty sunsets and forty full Earth rotations since James got hit by the brick.

I read in the S encyclopedia that the solstice marks the turning point, and after that, the days begin to grow longer. But I can tell that without looking at a calendar. I see the tiny black flecks Mom calls snow fleas appear in the few melting puddles of snow left in the yard. I feel the heat in the sun that rises over Bower Hill Road.

The meteorite is also the same, but different. It's camouflaging itself the way wild hares turn white in the winter and brown in the spring. Old, dead leaves blow up against it, filling in around the crater. The big rock is a favorite perch for the sandhill cranes, and the stone is spotted with bird poop. Squirrels run up the rock and eat the seeds out of scavenged pinecones, leaving the rest in little heaps. When I rub away the dirt and poop that collect on the rock, I can still see the shine of the surface, but from a distance the stone blends into the field and woods around it.

It's warm enough that ladybugs hatch in the house, and the sap runs in the big sugar maples. Cool nights, warm days, Mom says, make the sap move. She's boiling it down on a potbelly stove on Nana's porch. The stovepipe juts out so the smoke rises away from the house.

"Fly away, Babygirl," Birdie tells her baby doll, and throws it up in the air. Its yellow dress puffs out for a second and it drops to the ground.

James adds stovewood to the fire. His shaved hair is growing back.

"Henry, did you ever memorize that scientist's phone number?" he asks.

"No, I didn't, but I still have his card," I say, and that reminds me I've been wanting to call Dr. Morgan.

James surprises me with the things he forgets and the things he remembers. I think part of his memory is like the dark side of the moon. Forty-one percent of the moon, the dark side, is impossible to see, but we know it's there. I know there's no way to figure out a percent for James's memory.

I go inside and find my notebook. It opens to the page of questions where I tucked Dr. Morgan's card.

Is the meteorite the core of a destroyed planet?
Or is it a little piece of the core?
If there was ever a way to see and touch a part
of Earth's core, would it look anything like the
meteorite?

I study the phone number below his name on the card.

2-1-2-7-6-9-5-1-O-O

I dial Dr. Morgan's number. A woman answers on the second ring.

"American Museum of Natural History, how may I direct you?"

"I don't know. I'm not going anywhere. I'm calling for Dr. Miles Morgan, the curator. This is Henry Bower."

"One moment, please. I will try to put you through to his extension."

There is silence, then the phone rings once, twice, and a familiar voice comes on and says, "Miles Morgan speaking."

"This is Henry," I say.

"Henry! I am so pleased to hear from you. How have you and your lovely family been faring?"

It's hard to know where to start.

"We are good. Birdie says sentences now. She still likes red but she likes yellow, too. Also, Nana's hands are better, so she's going to pick dandelions greens to can this spring."

"Excellent. Please send my warmest regards to your grandmother," Dr. Morgan says.

"A bad thing happened, though. James got hit in the head with a brick and didn't wake up for a long time. Then I visited him and dripped some of what you called the rainbow water in his mouth and poured it on his head and he woke up that night. He's better, but he doesn't always remember everything the way he used to."

"Those are extraordinary developments indeed. I hope your mate James continues to improve."

"Me too. He's homeschooling with me now, but we might both go to school in the fall. Also, a flock of rare sandhill cranes are living down by the water. Braggy painted a sign on a wooden door with a picture of a crane, and now all these people are paying him to paint cranes on their front doors. He even got his picture in the newspaper. They called him a natural wildlife artist."

"Your uncle Braggy is indeed a man of many talents!"

"There's another bad part. I'm really sorry, but I lost the stone you gave me, the one from Nottingham. I put it on the drill bit of the drilling rig, and when the bit came up it was gone. I think it drew up the water, because we hit the biggest gusher my uncle Lincoln ever saw, and now the town has all the water it needs. I dowsed for it myself."

"I wouldn't call that lost, Henry. You used the stone for a good cause. In fact, I would call it a very successful scientific experiment. And it doesn't surprise me that you have the gift of divining."

I remember the main reason I called the curator.

"I decided I want you to take pieces of the rock to study at your museum. Maybe you can find out how it brings the water. So you could help places that have no water and make sick people better. And you could do that experiment you told me about, where you figure out how old a meteorite is."

"That's a very generous offer. We've had good success lately cutting meteorites with lasers. I don't expect we would need more than a small fraction of your stone, and we would leave the rest of it where it fell. First, though, I would like to invite you and your family to come to New York City and meet the team of scientists here. You could see the laboratory where we would take the pieces of your stone and see the equipment we use to study and test them. You would also get a private tour of our meteorite collection, including several rare specimens from the moon and Mars."

"Can James come, too?"

"Absolutely."

"We could see the Ahnighito."

"Certainly. I will be very interested in your impressions of the Ahnighito. Speaking of which, when I reference *your* meteorite to my team, what shall I call it? Have you come up with a name?"

The answer comes out of my mouth as if I knew it all along.

"Hat. Birdie named it the first time she saw it. You can tell your team it's called Hat."

"Hat," Miles Morgan repeats. "That's quite appropriate. I will share that moniker with my team. Also, please tell your parents to expect a letter with all the relevant information about a possible visit. For instance, we have a residence reserved for visiting scientists where you and your family can stay, and a museum fund to cover travel expenses."

"Thank you, Dr. Morgan, I will look for your letter in the mailbox."

Just as I hang up the phone, there's a sudden rainstorm. I go back out on the porch. The rain smells like the big rock mixed with the sweet smell of boiling sap.

I think about all the things that came to Bower Hill: the meteorite, the new stream, and the sandhill cranes. Bower Hill is the same but it's different. We're revolving around the sun five hundred and eighty-four million miles every year. The universe is too big to imagine, but from all that distance, it brought me a stone from the sky.

AUTHOR'S NOTE

What are the chances of finding a rock from space?

Henry's uncle Lincoln would probably say the chances of discovering a rock from space (a meteorite) are 50 percent, either you will or you won't! I've never found a meteorite myself, although I always keep an eye out for one. They're easiest to spot in sandy deserts or on the snow in polar regions. It's possible that you might see one fall to Earth. Or a meteorite could already be lying in your backyard or field or city street.

Are the Hoba and the Ahnighito real meteorites?

Yes! The iron Hoba meteorite, the largest one ever found, fell in Namibia, Africa, and weighs sixty tons. Because it was so heavy, it was never moved from where it fell. The Ahnighito, named "Tent" by the Inughuit, the people of northern Greenland, is the third-largest meteorite. It collided with Earth about 10,000 years ago, weighs thirty-four tons, and is made of iron-nickel alloy. It is on exhibit at the Arthur Ross Hall of Meteorites in the American Museum of Natural History in New York City. Visitors are able to see and touch its fusion crust and the two polished spots on its surface.

Many Inughuit feel the Tent/Ahnighito meteorite was taken from them by Admiral Peary without their consent, and they wonder what the economic situation in the area might be today if the meteorite had remained in the region. There is also the sad and disturbing history of the Inughuit people brought to New York City, along with the meteorite. Their stories can be found in the books *Give Me My Father's Body* and *Minik: The New York Eskimo: An Arctic Explorer, a Museum, and the Betrayal of the Inuit People* by Kenn Harper.

Could a meteorite cause a flood?

Whether a meteorite could ever draw water from the ground is not known—that's where I let my imagination take flight when writing this book. But some scientists believe most water on Earth was first brought here by asteroids and comets hitting the planet.

Could a space object from outside our solar system ever land on Earth?

In 2017, 'Oumuamua (Hawaiian for "a messenger from afar arriving first"), the first object from another star, was observed. It was shaped unlike anything seen before in space, ten times as long as it was wide (think of a pencil shape half a mile long and wider than a house!), with an orbit that was not bound by the sun's gravity. It was thought to be traveling through the Milky Way for hundreds of millions of years before it came into view. It didn't collide with Earth and was only visible for a short time before it continued on its journey.

In 2019, 21/Borisov, the first interstellar comet, arced across our solar system. Scientists think it may have originated around a red dwarf star, a much smaller and dimmer star than our sun.

Neither 'Oumuamua nor 21/Borisov came close to Earth, but it raises the possibility that a piece of another star system could one day make its way here.

Does dowsing really work?

Where I live, out in the country in Maine, many homes don't have access to a public water supply. Many of us have to develop our own water system. Some people get a backhoe operator to dig them a shallow well. Other people hire a drilling rig like Henry's father's to bore deep into hard granite to reach water from an aquifer.

When you don't have water, one of the things you do is spend a lot of time thinking about how to get it. Over the years, our dug well often went dry in late summer, and my family had to haul water from a nearby spring for two grown-ups, two children, two horses, and a pony! And horses drink five to twenty times more water in a day than people do.

When a dowser finally dowsed us a new deep well, we didn't hit a gusher, but luckily our well has never run dry.

Are you a dowser? Or do you have another gift? You'll never know until you try to use it, so I hope you do!

ACKNOWLEDGMENTS

With gratitude to Steven Chudney, who is 100 percent the best agent. Thank you for all you've taught me and for your dedication.

It's a dream come true working with editor Phoebe Yeh. From our first conversation, I was so excited by your vision for the book. Thank you for encouraging me to dig deeper and for knowing just what was needed.

With deep appreciation to the rest of the team at Crown Books for Young Readers who helped bring this book into the world, Elizabeth Stranahan and Melinda Ackell, and to Robert Frank Hunter and Katrina Damkoehler for the gorgeous cover and beautifully inspired book design.

To Dr. Denton S. Ebel, curator (meteorites), American Museum of Natural History, New York—thank you so much for sharing your knowledge about meteorites and space.

Writers Cathy McKelway, Sally Stanton, and Melanie Ellsworth, the greatest critique partners ever, for all your support.

A special thanks to early reader Greta Limberger.

And to anyone who has ever looked at a rock and wondered what it was made of and where it came from, or looked at the sky and tried to imagine what was out there beyond our sight and reach.

ABOUT THE AUTHOR

Betty Culley's debut YA novel in verse, *Three Things I Know Are True,* was a Kids' Indie Next List Top Ten Pick and an ALA-YALSA Best Fiction for Young Adults nominee. Her first middle-grade novel, *Down to Earth,* is inspired by her fascination with meteorites, voyagers from another place and time. She's worked as a pediatric nurse and lives in a small town in central Maine.

bettyculley.com